Praise for Omega Beta Monster

"A totally rad romp through 90s nostalgia, Greek myths, and college culture. I had so much fun getting to know these frat boys and their captivating monsters."

-Goldy Moldavksy, New York Times bestselling author of *The Mary Shelley Club*

"A harrowing adventure filled with twists and turns you won't see coming."

-John Ward, author of the Scareville series

"My favorite entry in the Totally Freaked! series yet. The writing is very much in the vein of Stine/Pike, and I could easily picture this on the shelf beside their names. Pledge this one onto your TBR... unless you want to possibly face Scylla's wrath."

-A.D. Aro, author of the Bumps in the Night series

TOTALLY FREAKED!

ΩMEGA BETA
MONSTER

AudraKate Gonzalez

MADAXEMEDIA.COM

Copyright © 2026 by AudraKate Gonzalez

All rights reserved.

No part of this publication may be reproduced, distributed, or transmitted in any form or by any means, including photocopying, recording, or other electronic or mechanical methods, without the prior written permission of the publisher, except as permitted by U.S. copyright law. For permission requests, contact info@madaxemedia.com.

This book is a work of fiction. Any references to historical events, real people, or real places are used fictitiously. Other names, characters, places, and events are products of the author's imagination, and any resemblance to actual events or persons, living or dead, is entirely coincidental.

Published by Mad Axe Media

madaxemedia.com

The Totally Freaked! series is an original creation of Mad Axe Media.

Edited by Joey Powell

Book Cover & Interior Design by Joey Powell

Print ISBN: 978-1-966497-12-7

E-Book ISBN: 978-1-966497-13-4

To Sarah Michelle Gellar, who had me answering the phone with "Omega Beta Zeta" for a long time.

ΩMEGA BETA
MONSTER

Buffy the Vampire Slayer
Season 2. Episode 5.
"Reptile Boy"

Xander Harris: So, Cor, you're datin' college guys, now?

Cordelia Chase: Well, not that it's any of your business, but I happen to be dating a Delta Zeta Kappa.

Xander Harris: Oh, an extra-terrestrial. So that's how you get a date after you exhausted all the human guys.

Chapter One

The heads of the Hydra stared at Miles from every direction. He couldn't seem to catch his breath. It was magnificent, but deadly. It could strike at Miles at any moment, killing him with one bite. Those razor-sharp teeth digging into his flesh. Crunching on his bones. Swallowing him. Straight down its gullet and into the belly of the beast.

"Pretty awesome, right?" Miles' dad, Jesse Sr., or Jess for short, asked as he approached the hydra.

Miles gazed at the stone fountain. "Yeah, it is pretty awesome." It sat at the center of the cul-de-sac like a centerpiece on a table. The fraternity and sorority houses lined the street all the way around the fountain. Water shot out from one of the mouths of the hydra, spraying Miles' freshly frosted hair with mist as it landed in the pool at its base. The plaque attached to the stone said that it was dedicated to the chapter of Omega Beta Mu, the extra-large sorority house—er, mansion—that rested directly behind the Hydra.

Miles' mom set one of his duffel bags on the sidewalk next to them. "It hasn't changed much," she said as she glanced around Greek Row. "It brings back so many great memories." She stood on her tiptoes to plant a kiss on Jess' cheek.

Miles groaned.

Of course his parents would have to take a moment to reminisce about the place. After all, they were alumni of Greek Row. His dad had been a part of Alpha Xi Pi while his mom was also part of one of the chapters. She didn't talk about it much, though. Whenever she did talk about Greek Row it was always about meeting his dad and how they fell in love, which Miles never liked to hear about. Super gross.

Miles was hoping that this day would be about him. That he would get his parents' recognition for pledging. For becoming a legacy. He was going to do his best to make them so proud.

"Jesse, can you help with one of these bags?" his dad asked Miles' younger brother.

"Yeah, sure, totally." Jesse walked right past the bags, too focused on playing his Game Boy to actually help. That was how Jesse always was: Too preoccupied in his own world to care, and their parents never said anything about it. Jesse was beyond spoiled. Never lifting a finger and always getting what he wanted. And he somehow ended up getting to be the Junior of the family, having the privilege of being named after their dad. It always bugged Miles since he was the firstborn, but he never spoke up about it.

Seeing that Jesse wasn't going to listen to their father, Miles picked up another bag, hiking it up on his shoulder.

Miles' mom leaned over and kissed Jesse on the forehead, ruffling his hair in the process.

"Daphne, leave our son be. He doesn't need you fumbling over him. You're going to embarrass him." Funny how they were worried about embarrassing Jesse but not Miles.

His dad walked right by Miles and toward the frat house.

Miles followed close behind. His dad knew exactly where they were going, but everything was a blur to Miles. Obviously, he'd toured the campus before and after being accepted, but the anticipation of becoming a part of it had his insides crawling with nervous jitters.

The entrance of Alpha Xi Pi was covered in Greek symbols and historical figures. A statue of a warrior loomed in the corner, a large sword at his side and a helmet decorated with feathers.

"Ares, god of war," his dad whispered in his ear. He then pointed to a serpent-like creature spread above the door frame leading to the commons. Miles could have sworn he saw one of the snakes blink in his direction, peering at him with a beady gaze. It startled him, and he backed up, bumping into his dad's burly chest. His dad must not have noticed the slight movement as he continued on. "That is Typhon. In Greek myths, he has one hundred snakes on his shoulders that can breathe fire. You wouldn't want to run into him in the dark." His dad let out a chuckle that sounded more like he was trying to cover a shaky breath.

Daphne sent a scolding glare in her husband's direction. "Well, Miles won't have to worry about running into *anyone* in the dark because he's going to obey *all* the rules. Aren't you?"

He nodded. "Totally."

The four of them climbed the grand spiral staircase to Miles' new living quarters: a twelve-by-nineteen room fit for three people.

Today would be the day that Miles would finally get to meet his new roommates in person. They were assigned weeks ago, but this would be their very first face-to-face interactions.

Miles had his fingers crossed that they'd be cool because Miles was determined to fit in with whatever "in crowd" existed on campus. He didn't need any dead weight cramping his style, and people could be cruel. Miles could be blacklisted just by association. A risk that Miles was not willing to take. He didn't spend his high school years being ignored, only to have the same thing happen at college.

To his surprise, when they reached the room, someone was already in there. Miles and his parents were early for drop off because his mom wanted to make sure he could show that he was more than punctual. He wasn't expecting one of his roommates to be just as punctual.

The walls were covered in freshly hung posters featuring bands like Nirvana, Pearl Jam, and Oasis.

A bulky TV rested on the edge of a dresser, and the sound of Beavis and Butthead's laughter reverberated off the bare windows.

Miles smiled. This was a good sign.

In the center of the room, struggling to make his bed, was a guy who appeared to be the same age as Miles. His dark hair hung by his shoulders. He wore a Chicago Bulls jersey with slouchy jeans. Miles recognized the jersey number as Michael Jordan's.

The guy stopped fidgeting with his fitted sheet when he spotted Miles and his parents standing in the doorway.

"Oh, hey, roomie, and uh … family." He held out his hand, and Miles shook it. "I'm Phinn."

At that moment, a box came barrelling into Miles' back, knocking him into the room the rest of the way. His parents let out loud gasps at the shock. Hidden behind the box was another guy.

"Oof, sorry about that!" He threw the box on one of the remaining empty beds. "I'm Derek." An incredibly tall, wiry-framed guy shook Daphne's hand. A look of disgust crossed her face when a brown substance transferred from Derek's hand to hers. "Yikes, chocolate from earlier. Got a little melted while I was trying to eat, but the sugar keeps me going." He shrugged. "Diabetic."

Miles' mom wiped her hand on her side. "Well, it's very nice to meet you both. I hope that you'll get along well with Miles." She walked over to place Phinn's fitted sheet on his bed. What a mom thing to do.

Miles sheepishly waved. "Hey, I'm Miles. These are my parents and my little brother. Who were just leaving, by the way." Miles gave them a head nod toward the door.

His dad purposefully deepened his voice for a more authoritative effect. "Mr. and Mrs. Pappas."

Phinn and Derek stood at attention. "Nice to meet you," they said in unison.

"And where might *your* parents be?" his mom asked.

"Mom," Miles said her name like a warning. They were freshmen in college. In a fraternity on Greek Row. They didn't need their parents breathing down their necks. In fact, Miles now regretted letting his parents even walk him up to his new place. He could feel the redness creeping up to his freckled cheeks.

"My mom and dad had to book it back to the city. I've got three other siblings at home that can't be left alone for too long. They'll tear the house down." Phinn chuckled.

"My parents couldn't get the day off, so it was a drop-and-go situation." Derek shrugged.

Miles raised his eyebrows at his parents. "Well, my folks can't stay either, right? Don't you guys have that thing going on today?"

His mom was about to protest, but his dad caught the hint to leave in Miles' tone.

"Yeah, that thing, right, dear?" His dad steered his mom by the shoulders toward the door.

"Why don't you walk us out, Miles?" Daphne asked.

He reluctantly walked them downstairs and to the front door. The whole way, his mom went over dos and don'ts'. "You listen to whatever those in charge tell you, okay?"

They'd finally reached the front door.

"Okay, Mom, I will."

She turned to Miles. "This place is very important to your father and me. Do your best to leave a good impression. Obey the rules. Even when you *really* don't want to."

Miles didn't like how his mom's voice sounded. Something hidden beneath it. But he shrugged it off as just her being emotional.

Miles received hugs and kisses and waved goodbye to his parents. Jesse barely muttered a "goodbye" before hopping in their minivan. Miles couldn't help but feel a little annoyed thinking that Jesse was getting exactly what he wanted; their parents all to himself. Not that their parents paid much attention to Miles anyway. The firstborn versus the baby. That's how it would always be.

Miles shut the door, turned on his heel, and his gaze travelled up to the figure of Typhon. Its empty golden eyes reflected the sunlight coming in from the window, giving it an odd glare. A chill ran down Miles' back. He took a deep breath and stepped forward. The echo of his footsteps became a whispered warning. Miles was on his own now, beginning a new adventure, making his parents proud, ready to live his dream. But something in the air quietly nagged at him, trying to tell him that dreams could easily transform into nightmares.

Chapter Two

"I'm starving. Why the heck do we have to come to this stupid thing anyway?" Derek chomped down on a snack-sized chocolate bar, smacking his lips together as he spoke. The sound was obnoxiously loud in the otherwise quiet evening. It made Miles lose his appetite.

Well, that wasn't the only reason Miles felt like he'd puke at the sight of food. His stomach churned with dread. Miles and his new roommates were on their way to their deaths.

Not really.

Miles just let his anxiety believe that.

The boys were really on their way to the grand Omega Beta Mu house for the start of the year kickoff. This event was where all the students would get together to meet the other sorority and fraternity houses to mingle and party. This would be Miles' moment to impress his fellow peers and hopefully stand out in a good way. No pressure.

"I bet they'll have plenty of food at the party. All college parties have plenty of food. It's like a given." Phinn looked up at Derek. "How do you stay so thin anyway?"

Derek shrugged his shoulders. "I don't know. Fast metabolism, I guess."

"Are you always hungry?" Miles asked.

"It's the diabetes. Type one. I've had it since I was a kid." He said it like it was no big deal, so Miles and Phinn didn't say anything else about it.

Miles fidgeted with the buttons on his striped linen shirt, unsure if he should button it all the way or leave a few undone. What would everyone else be wearing at the kickoff? He glanced at his roommates. Phinn remained in his jersey, but threw a relaxed blazer over it. The look shouldn't have gone together, but somehow on Phinn, it gave him an air of confidence.

He eyed Derek up and down. Derek had changed into what he worded as his "good clothes," but Miles thought they were anything but "good." Derek had a grunge style that, while looking awesome on someone like Kurt Cobain, looked ridiculous on Derek. Especially with melted chocolate mixed into the peach fuzz on his face.

Omega Beta Mu towered over them. It was shadowed by the lowering sun, and it somehow made it seem both inviting and intimidating. The front door was open. Laughter and chatter spilled out and flowed with the cool breeze.

The three boys marched up the marble staircase. It truly was the most beautiful house on Greek Row. It was also clearly the oldest house, made with brick and enormous pillars holding up the porch. The Greek letters for Omega Beta Mu hung above the large entrance.

Phinn and Derek walked through the open door and went ahead of Miles.

Miles took a deep breath before he stepped over the threshold.

A giant chandelier hung from vaulted ceilings. The floor was covered in lush red carpeting. It was straight out of a Hollywood movie. In the center of the entryway was a statue of a nude woman. She looked like an old crone. Dark lines dripped from her empty eyes while snakes entangled her hair. Bat-like wings gave her the appearance of being in mid-flight. There was a whip wrapped around her arm, and her mouth was open in a scream. If looks could kill, Miles would be dead.

"That's Alecto." A girl snuck up beside Miles, startling him. His breath caught. She was the most beautiful girl he'd ever seen. Her long blonde hair was so pale it was almost white, and combined with the porcelain of her skin, it made her lavender irises stand out. "She's an Erinyes."

Miles blinked at her.

"You know, a Fury?" The girl raised an eyebrow.

"Oh, yeah, Fury." Miles acted like he knew what she was talking about, but to be honest, even though Greek was his heritage, he had next to no knowledge about Greek history or the mythology.

The girl chuckled at him. "I'm Meghan." She held out a manicured hand, and he delicately shook it.

A few beats of Miles awkwardly shaking her hand, no words spoken, passed before he even realized he hadn't told her his name yet. Did he even know his name?

"Miles Franklin Pappas," he finally blurted out. His full name? Who gave their full name like that?

Her face flashed with intrigue. Or was that recognition? She wiped the look away quickly and replaced it with an award-winning smile as she released his hand. "Nice to meet you, Miles Franklin Pappas."

"You can call me Miles. I don't know why I said my full legal name. It's not like you needed to know it. It's just a habit, I guess." He was rambling.

"All right, Miles. You can call me Meg."

Miles started to shake the nerves from his body, bringing out the calm, cool, and collected version of himself. The version he had practiced in a mirror so many times prior to leaving the frat house. "You mean you're not going to offer me your full legal name? Address? Social security number? Seems only fair …"

A genuine laugh escaped Meg, and Miles could have bottled the sound. He was officially under her spell.

"That's usually only something I offer once someone's bought me dinner."

Another girl waved to Meg, interrupting their conversation and the smooth line that Miles was about to lay on her. Maybe it was his saving grace, though, in case Meg rejected him. Which was a very high likelihood considering they'd just met. He didn't want to come off as a complete weirdo.

"Well, I hope you enjoy your evening, Miles. There's hors d'oeuvres over there. The real party will start after chapter introductions." With that, Meg strutted away.

Derek walked over to Miles, a plate of vegetables in his hand. "Who was *that*?" he asked.

My future wife, Miles thought. "Her name is Meghan," was what he said instead.

"Everyone, gather 'round!" A girl with a tinkling voice spoke into a mic at the base of the grand staircase. It looked like it was the staircase to heaven. Or in this case, the staircase to Olympus. Next to her stood another girl who was signing everything she was saying. "Welcome to Greek Row!" Everyone cheered, fist pumping the air and howling. Miles, Derek, and Phinn joined in, throwing each other some high fives, too. "I'm Anya, and this is our interpreter, CiCi. Tonight is going to be filled with fun, music, dancing, and freedom!" More cheers erupted. The sound of glass shattered as some rowdy boys knocked into something. Whatever it was they broke must not have been important because nobody seemed to pay any attention to it.

Anya continued her speech. "But first, we'll start with chapter introductions." She did a little jump and clapped her hands in glee as she stepped away from the mic. They definitely picked the right girl to fill the place with enthusiasm.

The chapter introductions went around the room with each house leader announcing them into the microphone. After that, the floor was handed back to Anya. "Uh oh, it appears we still have one more introduction to make!" she shouted into the microphone, but then the lights went out and screams echoed around the room.

Chapter Three

The screams dwindled to whispers as soon as a spotlight illuminated the top of the grand staircase. Thumping music continued to pulse around the room, matching the frantic pace of Miles' rapidly beating heart in his chest. The stupid organ hadn't caught up with the knowledge that nothing terrible was taking place and that this was all part of the party festivities.

The DJ lowered the volume of the music.

Double doors swung open with a dramatic flourish, and two girls emerged. Miles' heart finally calmed and almost stalled when he saw that one of the girls was Meghan. The girl standing beside her was almost a mirror image–same cascading white hair, pale skin, and shocking lavender eyes. The only difference between the two was in the way they carried themselves. Meghan exuded a soft, sweet, and approachable nature, while the other girl radiated hard edges, sharpness, and assertive energy.

Hushed silence fell amongst the crowd as the two descended the stairs, their confident steps accentuated by the rhythmic click of their heels and the tantalizing glimpse of their long legs through the slits in their matching dresses. The spotlight followed their every move, casting a luminous glow that only emphasized their unnatural beauty and contrasting styles. Meghan's dress was pink with a fuzzy cardigan, while the other girl had chosen an inky black ensemble paired with a leather jacket.

Once they reached the mic, Meg gracefully stepped back into the shadows to give the other girl the spotlight.

The other girl stepped forward, her presence commanding the attention of everyone in the room. "Hello peasants," the girl spoke. Her husky voice was magnetic, drawing you in so that you would hang on every word she had to say.

Awkward chuckles followed her introduction.

Derek peered at Miles with raised eyebrows. A look of silent curiosity.

Meg, seeming to notice the tension of the crowd, elbowed the girl in the side.

She rolled her eyes. "I mean, hello, fellow students!" she exclaimed, softening her tone.

The crowd erupted in enthusiastic whoops and hollers.

"I'm honored to begin another year with all of you, both old and new members of Greek Row," the girl continued, her voice now a blend of excitement and authority. "My name is Alexandra Cronus, and this is my twin sister, Meghan."

Meg sheepishly waved, her cheeks changing rosy beneath the glow of the spotlight.

Alexandra pressed on. "Together, we are the chapter president of Omega Beta Mu, the oldest and most prestigious of all the houses on campus. The pride and joy of Greek Row." She paused for dramatic effect, waiting for her words to sink in to her audience. "Basically, if it wasn't for us, none of you would be here."

"Wait, two people can make up one president?" Phinn leaned in and asked Miles.

Miles may not have known a lot about Greek history, but he did know a lot about Greek life. He'd scoured every book and article he could find about Greek Row. His parents, when they weren't more interested in talking about how they met on campus, would also talk to Miles about Greek life and how important it was. Miles shook his head, his brows furrowed together. "This is the first time I'm hearing of something like that."

Alexandra's eyes darted in their direction. Miles saw a scowl painted on her face as though she was annoyed that they had the audacity to talk during her speech. Miles felt the weight of that glare, and though Phinn looked like he wanted to ask another question, the two boys both snapped their lips together.

Alexandra returned to her announcements. "Greek Week begins tomorrow, which I know you're all excited about!"

Miles joined in on the shouting. He knew all about Greek Week and how it was the kickoff week that would be filled with fun and friendly competitions.

"With that being said, I want to remind you that even though we are all part of separate chapters, what you do here as students reflects on Omega Beta Mu, which is why we are dedicated to making sure that *all* rules and expectations are upheld." Alexandra's gaze rested on Miles, her eyes penetrating through him. He squirmed beneath it, feeling like maybe she knew something about him that even he didn't know about himself. It was a strange thing to Miles that while he found Meghan's eyes so mesmerizing, Alexandra's just seemed wild to him.

"Which is where my sister comes into play. The rule police." Alexandra waved her arm, and Meg stepped up to the mic with an elegant stride.

"The rules and expectations are as follows." Meg's voice changed, trying to mimic the authoritative tone of her sister's, but it was still sweet and charming to Miles. "You are required to maintain a proper GPA of 3.5 or higher. You must regularly attend your chapter meetings and any other meetings being held that you have been invited to. Conduct yourselves inside and outside the campus in a respectable manner. Respect the property. We take confidentiality *very* seriously. Anything that takes place here is to be kept here. Our rituals, traditions, and internal matters are *private.* If anyone is found sharing outside of Greek Row, there will be consequences. Curfew hours are between midnight and six. During those hours, you are not to leave your houses."

Meg's voice echoed throughout the foyer, everyone paying attention to every rule and detail. Some of which was gone over during orientation, but hearing the rules come from Meg made them seem more important.

"With the exception of tonight!" Alexandra bumped Meg out of the way with her hip, bringing back a more lighthearted vibe to the room. "Tonight is meant for a good time, so there is no curfew in place. But we have one more announcement before we let the real party begin."

The lights came up, and music started to play. It was a song that reminded Miles of something out of a romcom that his mom would watch.

A group of girls now descended the staircase, all dressed up with makeup plastered on their faces. Each one held a red rose in their hands, the petals looking like velvet beneath the lights. They moved in unison. Their steps were all expertly choreographed.

The girls lined the stairs as Anya walked down the center of the steps with a large crystal cup cradled in her hands. Her movements were also deliberate and poised. She met a serene Meg at the bottom and passed her the crystal cup with a coy nod. Meg gently placed the cup on a pedestal next to the statue of Alecto.

"As some of you already know, every year we hold our favorite ceremony, and this year is no different." Alexandra paused to swipe her tongue across her red lips. "We are happy to announce this year's 152nd Row Bachelor contest!"

The announcement was met with the loudest roar of applause and cheers from previous members.

Guys in every direction hooted and hollered, banging on their chests like triumphant warriors, while others fist bumped their friends in a show of camaraderie. Miles, caught up in the wild frenzy, was pretty sure he saw one guy rip his own shirt off and flex his muscles. The spectacle was equal parts amusing and exhilarating as Miles mulled over the various possibilities of what Row Bachelor could be.

Row Bachelor wasn't something Miles had ever heard of. It wasn't anything his parents had ever talked about either, which meant that this contest must have been one of those sacred traditions that weren't allowed to be discussed outside of Greek Row.

"Shhhh, calm down, *gentlemen*." Alexandra smirked. Miles could tell she liked the attention. She soaked it up like a flower bathing in the sunlight. "For all of you freshmen out there who don't know, let's take a moment to discuss the Row Bachelor ritual. Every year, at the beginning of the school year, we hold what is known as Row Bachelor. This tradition began during the founding of the school in the 1800s and has continued ever since."

Alexandra took the microphone off the stand and began to slink around the room, eyeing every guy with a scrutinizing gaze. "Row Bachelor allows one lucky winner to experience living the life of a bachelor for a whole week. You will be doted on and treated like a king by none other than Omega Beta Mu, as you're hosted here, in our very home." She stopped and stood directly in front of Miles, Phinn, and Derek. "At the end of the seven days, a final ceremony will take place in your honor." She abruptly turned on her heels and stalked toward the cup resting on the pedestal. "All the boys on campus, regardless of year rank, are eligible to enter. You only need to enter by writing your name on a slip of paper and placing it into the crystal cup. The winner will be chosen at the start of Greek Week."

Meghan reached for the mic. "So, tonight at midnight."

Miles watched as the light glinted off the crystal cup. It was so enticing to him. The idea of getting to spend a whole week with Meghan? What could be better?

He eyed the room, though, feeling his heart sink along with his chances when he saw the amount of eager guys. They all wanted the opportunity, but only one of them could win.

"May the gods smile upon you." Meghan winked. Miles couldn't help but think the wink was meant for him. He was hooked.

"Now, let the party begin!"

Chapter Four

The main interior doors opened, and strobe lights zig-zagged in every direction. The bass thumped. Girls and guys alike gyrated against each other, moving their hips to the music. It was all so hypnotic.

And the celebration didn't stop there. Things had moved outside, too. Some people had stripped down into bathing suits and swim trunks to jump in the pool. Music reached the deck, and there were beach balls, pool noodles, and inflatable animals being thrown all about while people laughed and dunked each other under the water.

Miles spotted Alexandra making her way around to all the guys, whispering flirtatiously in their ears. She must have been encouraging them to enter the contest.

Miles didn't want to wait for Alexandra to come whisper sweet nothings in his ear. He knew exactly what he was going to do. He couldn't care less about the party. The line for the Row Bachelor cup was nearly out the front door. He'd already watched Phinn and Derek drop their names in, and a bunch of other guys too.

He wanted to get his name placed in the cup as soon as possible, but it felt like fate was against him because every time he got a little bit closer to dropping the slip of paper inside, a distraction popped up.

First, it was Phinn, begging Miles to play a round of pig with a group of guys from Alpha Xi Pi.

"Yeah, I'll play, just let me—" But before Miles could finish his sentence, he was being swept up by the swarm of basketball players out onto the court. And of course, when Miles saw that Meghan was outside watching the game, he couldn't quit. He needed to impress her.

After the game, it was Derek who needed help finding the bathroom.

Now, with no one else to grab his attention, it was the perfect time for Miles to drop his name in the cup.

The line was no longer full of guys. Many of them had already placed their slips of paper inside.

Miles hurried up and scribbled his name on a piece of paper, and headed toward the small line that remained. And then he was intercepted by Alexandra herself.

"Miles, enjoying the party?" She eyed him up and down.

Miles glanced around the room. It was beginning to empty as people moved further into the house and onto the dance floor or out to the pool. "Yeah, it's great!" He said over the music. Then it dawned on Miles that she'd called him by name. "How'd you know my name?"

"When my sister finds someone interesting, word gets around fast. Plus, you're a legacy. A Pappas."

Giddiness fluttered around Miles' stomach at the thought of Meg already mentioning him to her sister. This was a good sign in almost every young adult movie he'd ever seen. This was how one's popular status was born. This was how you got invited to future parties, sat at the "cool" table, and knew all the hot goss before everyone else did. Before Miles would know it, he'd be at the top of the popular pyramid.

"So, you know my family?" Miles asked.

Alexandra threw her head back in a laugh. "Of course I do. Your parents are both alumni. There are pictures of them from their years hanging all around the campus. In fact, your mom was once part of Omega Beta Mu."

"Really?" Miles always knew what chapter his dad was from, but his mom was so tight-lipped about what sorority she was part of.

"I can't believe you didn't know that. She never told you?" Alexandra's eyebrows raised.

"She never really talks about her time being in a sorority. She mainly talks a lot about how she and my dad met and how in love they were." Miles made a face to show his disdain.

"Yeah, real lovebirds."

"Huh?" Miles thought the way that Alexandra talked made it sound like she knew his parents. But that would be absurd ...

A familiar face appeared next to Alexandra, and Miles couldn't have been happier to see Meghan. She had changed, once again, and now she was in a bright neon bathing suit, her hair slicked high into a ponytail and secured by a green scrunchie that matched her suit.

"What are you two talking about?" she asked.

"Oh, just the fact that Miles had no idea his mom was in this sorority."

Meghan looked surprised.

"Wild, right?" Alexandra asked her sister.

A look passed between the two sisters that Miles could not decipher. But he wasn't able to think about the look too long because the next thing he knew, Meg was grabbing his hand.

"Why don't we go out to the pool for a swim. I'm dying to get out of this stuffy house." The Row Bachelor cup and any other thought Miles had disappeared as he followed Meghan's swishing ponytail outside. Her hand fit perfectly in his.

What if my hand is clammy, though?

Worried, Miles slipped his hand out of Meg's and nervously placed it in his pocket.

"Everything okay?" Meg asked.

"Oh, yeah, totally. I just–I–didn't think to wear my swim trunks." Miles felt like kicking himself. It's a freaking college party. He should have been prepared for anything.

Meg gave him a teasing grin. "That's okay. Do you wear boxers or briefs?"

Miles choked on his spit. "Wha–what?"

"Boxers or briefs?"

"B-boxers."

"Then no swim trunks, no problem." Meg did a little run and then cannonballed into the pool. Meg surfaced from the water. She whipped her head back, and her ponytail sprayed water in every direction. "Are you coming in? Or did you forget how to swim, too?" she teased.

Miles checked around the pool deck to make sure no one was looking. Everyone was so caught up in having fun with the pool noodles, beach balls, and inflatables that they couldn't care less what he was doing.

Miles tossed his clothes on a chair and jumped into the pool after Meg.

She giggled when he came up for air and splashed him with water. "Perfect form! I give it a solid 8."

"Only an 8?! Come on, I would give it at least a 9.5. You have to consider the size of the wave I produced," Miles joked.

"Ah yes, you did produce a nice wave."

"Thank you, thank you. Hold the applause, please." Miles gave a slight bow.

Meg splashed him with water. "I'm not changing my score, though. If you want a better one, you're gonna have to come and get it."

Before Miles could react, Meg dove beneath the water and into the depths of the pool. Sucking in a deep breath, Miles flipped his body and followed her down.

Only once he got beneath the water, there was no Meg in sight. In fact, there wasn't anyone. There were so many people in the pool when he had jumped in, but from down here, he couldn't see anyone swimming above. The whole pool seemed to just disappear around him.

Miles was surrounded by dark, open water.

Scared, Miles began to frantically swim upward. Something wrapped around his leg. He looked down to find an inky black tentacle secured around his calf. It tugged him down. A scream escaped Miles' throat, sending out a flourish of bubbles around him.

Miles kicked his legs, trying to propel himself up, but then another tentacle wrapped around his waist, dragging him even further below.

Miles reached down to pull at the tentacle, and he was met by a pair of glowing yellow eyes staring at him. He could make out a scaly woman, hair flowing wildly in the current, ringed by ten other tentacles around her. She smiled wickedly, revealing a set of sharp teeth.

The creature used its tentacles to pull itself closer to Miles.

Miles spun around and forced himself to swim as hard as he could. His lungs ached and burned. He was beginning to lose air. Another tentacle grabbed his arm, and he swore he could hear the creature laughing at him.

His ears painfully popped. Miles felt water pouring into his mouth. He couldn't hold his breath any longer. He gasped as the water filled him up. The monster would make a quick feast out of him for sure. Miles hoped he'd drown before he could feel its fangs rip into his flesh.

One more bubble escaped from between his lips before his entire body went limp in the grasp of the creature, and everything in Miles' world went black.

Chapter Five

Miles coughed up pool water next to him on the deck. It tasted like acrid chemicals on his tongue. His lungs ached, and his throat was on fire from the burning sensation of nearly drowning. As he finally managed to pry his eyes open, he was met with blurry, concerned faces hovering above him. Murmured whispers floated around the deck, wondering if he was okay, if he was alive.

"Oh, thank goodness!" Meg squealed, her voice slicing through the ripples of worry. "I thought we were going to have to call an ambulance."

"Good thing I know CPR," Phinn chimed in. He hoisted Miles up from the ground with surprising ease.

"I ran right over when I heard them pulling you out of the water."

Miles felt a little woozy. Phinn guided him to a lime green inflatable chair. The chair made an embarrassing fart noise when Miles' wet body slid down on it, eliciting a few chuckles from the group.

Meg threw a towel around his damp shoulders. "You should have told me you didn't know how to swim. I would have never dove under like that." Her words were laced with care, and something else that Miles couldn't quite make out. Whatever it was made her sound like she wasn't completely genuine, which bothered him.

Alexandra was standing in the crowd of onlookers. Miles could feel her eyes pinned on him as she watched the interaction between him and her sister.

Miles shivered as he dried himself. "I do know how to swim, but—" He stopped. What was he going to say? That he knew how to swim, but there was a giant octopus woman monster in the water that was trying to kill him? Yeah right. He clearly was hallucinating.

Maybe he needed to eat something. His stomach gurgled in response. He could really go for a ham sandwich with Nacho Cheese Doritos right about now …

"But what?" Meg asked, one eyebrow raised, her eyes narrowed.

Alexandra slinked in next to Meg as if she too wanted to hear what the cause for all the commotion was.

"I must have gotten kicked in the head when I went under. A lot of people swimming in the pool at the same time. Accidents happen."

"Yeah, accidents happen," Alexandra butted in, her head tilted to the side.

Miles really did not like her. There was something strange, something dangerous about her. Maybe she had wanted Miles to drown. Maybe she even knew about the octopus woman lurking in the pool.

Don't be ridiculous, Miles, he internally scolded.

"Well, I just came over to let you all know that the pizza has arrived," Alexandra announced. Miles could tell that wasn't the real reason she'd come over, but he wasn't going to call her out.

Meg left his side to retrieve his clothes. She held them out to him. "Let's get you dressed and get you some pizza."

With the help of Phinn steadying him, he redressed. The whole time he was trying to convince himself that he really did get kicked in the head.

The greasy, pepperoni-stuffed crust pizza from Pizza Hut did not disappoint. Miles ate six slices, which Derek picked on him for. Miles found that funny, though, considering he saw Derek eat plenty this evening. Miles didn't know where he put it, though. The guy was a walking stick.

"Where was your slice of pizza?" Miles asked Derek.

"Gotta watch my blood sugar. My levels are good right now. Don't want to spike it."

Miles burped. "Well, it was delicious." He rubbed his now bloated belly.

"Right, I could go for a nap after that." Phinn wiped his mouth with a napkin.

Derek yawned. "I'm down for a nap."

"Boys," Meg interjected, "there's no time for napping. The winner for Row Bachelor is going to be called soon!"

As soon as Meg said that, the microphone from the foyer was picked up by Alexandra. "Will all the guests please make their way to the entrance as we get ready to announce our lucky winner?!"

Miles' heart sank. He lost track of time, and now it was too late for him to be included in the contest. His eyes shifted over to Meg, watching as she cleaned up her plate. He hoped that even though she'd be spending a lot of time doting on the Row Bachelor, she'd still have time to hang out with him if he asked.

The foursome shuffled out to the entrance and observed as Anya carried the crystal cup to Alexandra. When she passed it off, Anya bowed. Miles found that to be an odd gesture. It wasn't like Alexandra was a queen. Although maybe she was. Queen Bee at least.

"And the winner of Row Bachelor is ..." Alexandra sunk her hand into the crystal cup and mixed it all around.

Everything moved in slow motion, and a thick fog rolled into the room.

Chanting voices that hovered above the room thundered in Miles' ears. He looked for the source of the voices. Maybe there was a hidden choir somewhere, or maybe some of his fellow peers knew some sorority alma mater that he didn't know, but everyone else was staring intently at the cup.

"*Thysía. Thysía. Thysía. Thysía.*" The strange word echoed throughout the room. Not a single mouth moved. The sound wasn't coming from the speakers either. It was like a ghost was reciting some incantation.

"Do you hear that?" Miles leaned over and whispered to Derek, but Derek blankly stared ahead as though Miles were invisible. His pupils had disappeared. White, creamy eyes glowed instead. In fact, the whole room was lit up by everyone's glowing eyes.

Miles waved his hands in front of Phinn's hypnotized eyes. "Hello? Earth to Phinn?" No response.

Miles couldn't understand what was happening. He spun in a circle, searching from person to person, shaking them, yelling at them, but it was as if they were all trapped under some kind of spell.

A wicked wind rushed through, knocking Miles to the floor. It sent Alexandra's hair spiraling behind her. And ... were Miles' eyes betraying him? He could have sworn that the wind had picked Alexandra up and that she was floating above the ground.

Red liquid boiled from within the crystal cup, splashing onto Alexandra's face, but she didn't seem to notice. It bubbled over the sides, sending a crimson wave sloshing onto the floor. A metallic scent filled the air, prickling Miles' nose. Blood.

"*Thysía. Thysía. Thysía. Thysía.*" The deep chant became more urgent. Miles felt the beat of a drum pound through the floors, shaking his very core.

And just as quickly as everything had begun, it swiftly ended, bringing the room and Miles back to speed. Into the present. As if none of it had happened and it was all in Miles' head.

"Miles Pappas," Alexandra's voice boomed. Everyone in the room parted, and they all turned to look directly at Miles. He was still sitting on his butt on the ground. He looked at his peers. They were no longer zombified.

Derek leaned down, clapping Miles on the back. "Dude, that's you."

Miles hesitantly nodded his head as he stood. Now on steady feet, everyone began to cheer for him.

Alexandra flashed him a sly smile, and Meg embraced him in a hug.

"Congrats, Bachelor," Meg whispered in his ear.

And while an excited bolt struck within Miles at the very notion that he was now Row Bachelor, a static feeling of uncertainty buzzed in his veins, because he knew that he hadn't put his name in that crystal cup.

Chapter Six

"It was the weirdest thing ever. To jump in the pool and then see a giant octopus monster ready to have me for a snack. A living nightmare, I swear." Miles sat a stack of books on a book cart. He didn't feel brave enough to say anything about the creature in front of Meghan or Alexandra, but Derek and Phinn were becoming fast friends. They were his roommates, so he felt safe sharing what he saw.

Derek picked up a stack of books. "You were starving, man. I guarantee it was just a hallucination from a lack of food. You're supposed to eat before you swim."

The three boys were spending the day in the library as part of their Greek Week community service. It was their job to reshelve books in the correct order, giving Miles a lesson on how the Dewey Decimal system worked. And even as someone who didn't read a bunch, he had to admit that the library was a fascinating place. They had books on every subject you could possibly imagine. Not to mention quite a few new PCs that had Windows 95.

"I thought the saying was 'wait to swim after eating'?" Miles looked at Derek quizzically.

"Dude, always eat before physical exertion." Derek's voice was serious.

Phinn rolled his eyes at them both. "Who cares about eating and octopus monsters? I don't know how that's the thing you're focused on when you're the freaking Row Bachelor."

Miles shook his head at that statement. "I don't know how I am. I'm telling you, I did *not* put my name in the cup."

"Well, somebody stuck your name in," Phinn said as he shelved some more books in the mythology section.

Derek must have seen that Phinn shelved one of the books wrong, so he swapped it around. "Ooh, maybe it was that Meghan girl. You two looked awfully close."

Miles could feel his cheeks turn red. "I highly doubt Meg put my name in the cup. That's probably against the rules. And you heard them during their speech. Meg is not a rule breaker."

"I bet she'd break the rules for you." Phinn waggled his eyebrows like they were doing the worm on his forehead. Derek burst out in laughter, and Miles punched them both in the arm with a chuckle.

"Ha-ha, very funny," Miles said.

One of the librarians, an older woman with bright orange hair, which was definitely not her natural color, and glasses, came around the corner and shushed them.

Phinn and Derek quickly went back to work at the sight of her.

"Sorry, ma'am," Miles apologized before joining the boys again in their duties.

Phinn moved some more mythology books around to make room for the stack that Miles held in his hands.

"What do you think the first Row Bachelor reward is going to be?" Derek asked.

"I have no idea," Miles answered.

"It should start today, though. I bet Omega Beta Mu is just waiting for the perfect time to surprise you."

Derek swayed a little on his feet, knocking over a stack of books.

Phinn caught his arm before he could tumble to the ground. "Sugar low?" Phinn asked.

"Must be." Derek reached into his pocket and pulled out a bag of Skittles. "I guess I didn't realize that putting books away would be a lot more physical than I thought."

Miles bent down to pick up the fallen stack of books. His heart leapt to his throat. One of the books was flipped open to a page of a creature that looked exactly like the octopus woman who tried to drown him.

His hands shook as he held the book.

"You okay, dude?" Derek asked. "You look a little pale."

Miles swallowed hard, trying to keep his voice steady. "You guys aren't going to believe this, but this is *exactly* what I saw in the pool last night!" he whispered harshly, pointing to the illustration in the book. Derek and Phinn gathered around him and looked at the opened book. "Scylla, the man-eating monster," Miles read the description beneath the picture.

"Miles, don't be ridiculous." Phinn closed the book, revealing the title on the cover. "This is Homer's

Odyssey. It's a piece of literature. Not real life. I think Greek Life really is getting to your head."

Derek chuckled. "I don't know, Phinn. The book is shelved in the nonfiction section." His voice dripped with sarcasm.

Phinn smirked at Derek before the two boys both burst out in laughter. But Miles didn't join in on their outburst. He was laser-focused on the image. Goosebumps trailed up his arms as he remembered the way the slimy tentacles wrapped around him, pulling him ever closer, ever deeper. How his lungs burned, begging for air. The terrifying, razor-toothed smile of the monster.

Miles had almost convinced himself that it didn't happen. That it wasn't real. But seeing the picture of Scylla only made him realize that he couldn't lie to himself anymore. He saw this thing in the depths of the pool, and it had tried to kill him.

Chapter Seven

Miles stood in front of the mirror, examining the polo shirt and cargo pants he'd chosen, the memory of Scylla pushed to the back of his mind. Not forgotten. No, he made sure to check out the copy of Homer's *Odyssey* before he left the library. The book was now stacked on top of his current textbooks.

He popped the collar of his shirt like he'd seen so many other guys on campus do. He thought he looked presentable enough for an evening out.

When the boys had finished up at the library, one of the girls from Omega Beta Mu stopped by, displaying a playful smile and handing Miles a pink note, covered in lipstick prints, that had instructions on what to wear and what time to be ready by. He wasn't sure what the surprise was, but the anticipation was killing him.

A crash resounded behind him.

Phinn had thrown his controller down. "Dang it! I can't believe you beat me again!"

Derek shrugged, a smug look on his face. "Don't feel bad, Phinny boy. I've been playing the game a lot longer than you have."

Miles plopped down on the bean bag chair next to them. "The game has only been out for a week."

Derek and Phinn were going head to head in the new *Goldeneye 007* video game for Nintendo, and Derek had already bested Phinn in three rounds of *You Only Live Twice*.

"And I've put plenty of hours in on this bad boy. My mom swears it's going to rot my brain, which is why she made me promise to leave it at home along with my Nintendo. And I did promise. But I also had my fingers crossed." Derek began a new game, but when a loud *honk* shook the walls of their frat room, all three boys hopped up from their bean bags and ran to the window.

Parked out front was a long Cadillac Limo with blacked-out windows and chrome embellishments.

The moonroof on the top opened, and Meg popped up from inside.

"Hey, Bachelor!" she yelled, waving at Miles. "Come on down! It's time for your first night of pampering!"

Miles' roommates excitedly swatted at his arms while Miles all but tripped over his own two feet trying to run out of the room. He bolted down the stairs and didn't slow down until he reached the front door. With one sweaty palm on the handle, he took his other hand and swept it through his hair, making sure his frosted spikes were still in place, took a deep breath, and opened the door.

Meg was now standing at the door of the limo. She wore a black floral dress with platform sandals. Her hair was delicately pinned up, loose curls hanging down, with gold butterfly clips sparkling in the setting sun.

"Ready for your first night as Bachelor?" she asked.

"Absolutely," was the only word Miles could manage. Even though he was Row Bachelor, he wanted to make sure that he treated Meg like a gentleman. He wanted to show her what it would be like to date someone like him, and tonight would be a good start at showcasing that.

He jogged to her side and grabbed the door to the limo before she could, opening it and motioning her inside. When she was safely seated, Miles closed the door. He went to the back of the limo. On the trunk of the limo, there was a three-headed dog made of chrome. It made Miles smirk. While his Greek knowledge was limited, Miles did know about Cerberus. His childhood beagle bore the name because his dad thought it would be funny. Beneath the chrome dog was a license plate that read "Styx."

"You coming?" Meg's head was peeking through the moonroof again.

Miles moved around the limo and got in on the other side of Meg. He wasn't expecting to see that it was just him and Meg. He'd thought for sure that more girls from Omega Beta Mu would show up to be a part of the first surprise.

The driver started the engine, and they were off.

Miles drummed his fingers on his leather seat. "This is part of Row Bachelor, and not a–"

"A date?"

Miles choked on his saliva, not able to respond.

Meg laughed at him. "Don't worry, Miles. It's part of Row Bachelor. It was Alexandra's idea. She thought we really hit it off at the party, and that you might have more fun if it was just lowkey for the first surprise."

"And a limo is lowkey?" Miles raised his eyebrow.

"Daddy said I could borrow it for the night."

Daddy? So this was their limo? Figured the Cronus sisters were rich.

"Where are we going?" Miles asked.

Meg reached over and grabbed an ice-cold bottle of soda, pouring it into a champagne flute. She handed the glass to Miles and poured one for herself. He noticed a box of pizza resting on the seat across from them. It smelled like pepperoni, Miles' favorite.

"We're going out for a night on the town to the movies. It'll be fun!" Meg sipped her drink. "You know, I'm really glad it was your name that was drawn."

As happy as that made Miles feel, he needed to be upfront with Meg. Honesty was good, especially being honest with a girl you were interested in. "I'm glad too, but I have to tell you, I never put my name in the cup." He didn't know why, but his heart pounded in his chest as he waited for her response. What if his honesty stripped him of his title as Row Bachelor?

Meg clucked her tongue, all of a sudden finding her manicure very interesting. She examined each nail like an explorer reading a map, avoiding his gaze. Finally, two words flitted out between her lips. "I know." A mischievous glint flickered in her eyes.

The air became stale. The lush interior suddenly felt smaller. Silence entered the back of the limo as Miles absorbed those two words, turning them over and over in his head.

She knows?

Chapter Eight

"Was it you?" Miles twisted in his seat, the leather creaking beneath him, to look Meg in her lavender eyes. Maybe his roommates were right after all.

There was another beat of silence, the hum of the limo filling the space, before she answered. "No." Miles' heart sank a bit. "It was fate." Meg scooted closer to him, her voice slipping into a whisper. "The gods wanted it to be you, so they made it happen."

Obviously, Meg was really into the belief in gods. But Miles knew that there wasn't a collection of celestial beings making sure that it was his name chosen so he could hang out with the prettiest girl on campus. Although maybe it sounded like the work of something Cupid would do.

Miles chuckled at that thought, and Meg gave him a curious glance.

"It's nothing," Miles responded.

He was confused, though. Somebody on campus wanted to make sure his name got put in the cup. There were a slew of other guys at the party who were itching at the chance to be Row Bachelor.

"Are you sure?" Meg asked.

"Not trying to crush your whole 'fate' theory, but I know somebody physically put my name in the cup. I just wonder who?"

"Who cares? I'm glad somebody did." A reddish hue snuck up onto Meg's cheeks, the rosiness matching the flowers on her dress. "I like you, Miles. You seem like a fun guy."

Shock hit Miles from both sides—one side shocked at Meg's admission to liking him, and the other side shocked that she's not just a little curious as to who put his name in for the drawing.

"You like me?" He wished his voice didn't come out all high and squeaky.

But Meg didn't expand on the subject any further. The limo stopped right outside the front of the theater.

The privacy window from inside the limo rolled down. The driver turned around in his chair. He was like a ghostly figure straight out of a black and white horror film. He wore one of those chauffeur caps and a black suit. He was old with a long, stringy, gray beard. His eyes were pale blue, so pale they were almost silver, as if they had faded over time, blending in with the whites of his eyes.

"We've arrived." The driver's voice was hoarse, a gravelly, ancient sound. It rattled around in his throat like old chains. Miles wondered how long this guy had been driving. Probably since horse-drawn carriages were a thing.

"Thank you, Char," Meg chirped, and then she grabbed Miles by the arm, and together they walked into the theater before Miles could stare at the man any longer.

Rain pitter-pattered on the marquee of the theater hanging over Miles and Meg's heads. They were waiting for Char to make it back around with the limo. Miles inhaled the scent of the precipitation. He loved that smell.

"So, what did you think of the movie?" Meg asked. She popped a Jujyfruit into her mouth. She'd bought the box of candy from the concession stand on their way out. Her teeth smacked up and down loudly on the gummy morsel. If it were anybody else chewing like that, Miles would have been set on edge by the sound. But with Meg it was different. She could do anything, and it wouldn't bother him. Even during the movie, when she slurped on the drink they shared and unleashed a burp that could have rivaled a monster truck, instead of Miles being grossed out or embarrassed, he was genuinely impressed. The burp was a gnarly one, truly of epic proportion, and he fist bumped her for the display.

The burp was also a nice distraction from the movie. They ended up seeing *Mimic*. Miles didn't know much about the film going in. He hadn't seen the trailer for it prior. But it ended up being a horror film about cockroaches evolving due to an experiment gone wrong. It had Miles squirming in his chair the whole time.

"It was good," Miles said, trying to sound convincing.

Meg cocked her head in his direction. "Miles, be honest. Did it scare you?"

Miles shook his head, feigning nonchalance.

"Come on now. The giant bugs crawling everywhere? The way they began to look and sound human? The blood and guts?" For added effect, Meg took her fingers and tickled them up and down his arms to imitate the feeling of bugs wriggling over his skin. It made Miles shiver.

He couldn't take the sensation anymore. He playfully swatted at her hands. "Okay, okay. I surrender. The movie made me a *little* uncomfortable."

Meg gave him a satisfied smirk.

The headlights of the limo shone through the raindrops. Like before, Miles let Meg in first before getting in on the other side. He shut the door and saw that Meg was frantically searching all around the seat.

"Oh no!" Meg exclaimed in dismay. "I must have left my purse in the theater." She cracked her door open.

"I can go get it for you." Miles offered, leaning forward.

"No, that's okay. I think I know just where I left it."

And before Miles could protest any further, she was out of the limo and darting back into the building.

Inside the limo was quiet except for the drumming raindrops that pelted against the roof. Minutes passed by, each one longer than the last, until it had been too many minutes. Miles figured that Meg would have found her purse by now, but maybe she needed help.

Miles reached for the door handle. There was a click, and he saw the lock to the door slip beneath the frame, sealing him inside. He jiggled the handle. Pressed his body up against the door. Threw his weight against it to force it open. Miles looked down to see that there were no buttons that would allow him to unlock the door himself. He knocked on the privacy window. "Hey, Char, mind letting me out?" He called to the driver, his voice a mix of concern and desperation. But rather than responding to Miles' plea, Char revved the engine, shifted to "drive," and squealed the limo away from the curb at rapid speed. The unexpected force of the vehicle taking off threw Miles back against his seat. He smacked his head hard against the headrest with a sickening thud. Stars danced across his vision.

The world outside of the limo raced by them in a chaotic blur of images, swirling and twirling until it was just blobs of lights and colors. With panicky hands, Miles searched for a seatbelt but couldn't find one. He gripped the edges of his seat, his knuckles turning white as he held on for dear life. The limo swerved and weaved erratically.

"Char!" he shouted in fear. "What are you doing?! Slow down!" His words were swallowed by the shriek of the engine and the rush of wind and rain outside.

To Miles' growing dismay, Char didn't slow down. Instead, Char spun in his seat to face him, leaving the limo to drive itself. Miles watched in horror as the steering wheel seemed to be controlled by invisible hands.

The privacy window separating them rolled down with a hiss. A thick cloud of smoke unfurled from the front cab, billowing and piling into the back. Sweat pooled down Miles' forehead, the limo becoming as hot as an oven. The pungent smell of sulfur burned Miles' nose, stinging his nostrils and making his eyes water. He felt as if he was being cooked alive. Like he was trapped in a metal coffin hurtling out of control down the road.

Two gnarled hands pressed against the frame of the window. Through the swirling smoke, Char's ghastly face appeared. He coughed, and a sputter of dust rushed out of his mouth, followed by the most horrifying thing that Miles could have ever imagined. A swarm of cockroaches flew out of his open maw in a revolting buzz. Miles screamed, batting the insects away as they sped toward him. Some landed on his clothes, their spindly legs clinging to the fabric, while others climbed across his skin.

From Char's shriveled lips, a familiar chant spilled out. "*Thysia. Thysia. Thysia. Thysia.*" As he continued his chant, his face began to drip like candle wax in a blazing fire. Miles shut his eyes and shook his head, trying to erase what he thought he saw from his mind. Praying that it was all just a hallucination. But when he opened his eyes again, more of Char's face had melted away, revealing muscle and sinew beneath. The acrid smell of decay, adding to the already overwhelming stench of sulfur, was too much for his stomach. Miles yakked up vomit onto the floor.

"*Thysia. Thysia. Thysia. Thysia.*" Char contorted his body, warping it in an unnatural way. He cracked his bones and twisted his limbs at impossible angles so that he could climb through the window, inching closer to Miles with each jarring movement. The rest of Char's fleshy bits slopped off his form, landing in a slippery puddle on the plush carpet. Char was now a skeletal figure, his bones gleaming in the dim light. He reached his bony fingers toward Miles.

Miles pushed himself as far back into his seat as he possibly could, but there was nowhere else for him to go. No place for him to retreat to escape this terrible nightmare.

"THYSIA. THYSIA. THYSIA. THYSIA."

Miles covered his ears as the chant became a roar from Char's skull, vibrating throughout the car.

The driver's skeleton crawled up Miles' legs, stabbing his phalanges into his thighs.

"THYSIA. THYSIA. THYSIA. THYSIA."

And then Char grabbed the sides of Miles' head. Miles thrashed in his grasp, but the corpse firmly held him, his grip like a vice.

"THYSIA. THYSIA. THYSIA. THYSIA."

He squeezed Miles' face, forcing Miles to open his mouth. Char opened his jaw, and from the dark abyss of the driver's skull, Miles could see them. A writhing mass of fluttering cockroaches making their way to the surface. Making their way toward Miles' own mouth. Their antennae twitched with anticipation.

The cockroaches poured out of Char like a tide and surged into Miles. The bitter taste of the chitinous pests burst across his tongue. Hot tears escaped Miles' eyes as he choked on a scream tamped down by the skittering insect's bodies.

Chapter Nine

"Miles! Miiiiillllleesssss!"

A force shook Miles' arm, and his eyes flung open. His heart pounded in his chest as he shot up in the limo, his head bumping the ceiling, and frantically brushed at his mouth, tongue, and everywhere else on his body for cockroaches. His gaze met Meg's concerned lavender eyes.

"I didn't mean to startle you." She sat down in the seat as if nothing was wrong. As if Miles hadn't just experienced the limo ride from Hell. His head swiveled all around the vehicle. No cockroaches. No speeding down the road. No skeletal figure. They were back at the theater as though they had never left in the first place.

"Sorry it took me so long to find my purse. I thought I left it in the chair, but after looking around for a bit, I found out that someone had turned it into lost and found." She looked up at Miles, who was still standing up. "Did you have a nice nap?"

A nap? Did he have a nice *nap?*

Miles slowly sank down into the chair, shoulders slumped, completely embarrassed. He saw that the privacy window was up, Char sitting at the steering wheel. They pulled away from the curb and headed back to Greek Row. Of course he'd fallen asleep. And the cockroach skeleton nightmare? Obviously a concoction of his subconscious after seeing that movie.

Miles gave Meg a sheepish grin. "Sorry, I fell asleep. I thought about coming in to help you, but I guess I was more tired than I thought."

Meg playfully bumped his shoulder with her own. "No problem. Everything worked out exactly how it was supposed to."

The next night, Miles slept like a log. No more crazy nightmares. No monsters. No cockroaches. No octopus women. In fact, nothing else weird had happened in two days. And the Row Bachelor surprises? Totally awesome! Yesterday, the Omega Beta Mu group took Miles cosmic bowling. Neon lights, loud music, and Miles trying his best to impress Meg with his bowling game.

That was a strike in itself.

He lost to Meg. She accused him of letting her win, and he didn't let her think any differently. In reality, she kicked his butt. She had serious bowling skills.

The day before that was a trip to get ice cream and hang out at the park where the girls packed a nice picnic. They brought enough food to feed a small army. Sub sandwiches, Doritos, fruit, veggies, and plenty of Surge to drink.

All the girls from Omega Beta Mu were really cool and a blast to hang out with. But even surrounded by all those girls, Meg still gained all of Miles' attention. She was a spotlight, and Miles was a moth. The other girls seemed to notice and gave him and Meg their space from time to time. It was like they were all in some secret little rom-com.

Except for Alexandra. She was a different story, and Miles didn't know what to think of her. Not that he wanted her fawning over him like all the other girls, but she was one-half of the president. He assumed she would be more invested in treating Miles properly as Row Bachelor, but she acted more like he was a nuisance. She seemed to enjoy jumping at whatever chance she could to be condescending and passive aggressive with Miles. She either liked keeping him on his toes or watching him squirm.

And today was no different.

Miles was planted on the couch in the commons area of Omega Beta Mu, trying to look busy while waiting for Meg to get ready. He and a few other girls from the sorority were going roller skating tonight. Even cooler was that the girls told him he could invite some friends, so obviously he'd asked Phinn and Derek if they wanted to come, too. His roommates were more than happy to say yes to the invite. They were probably already on their way to the skating rink now.

Miles bounced his leg up and down while he flipped through the pages of Homer's *Odyssey*. As he read, there seemed to be a recurring theme of temptation throughout the story. The constant draw and pull of falling for pleasures like beauty, pride, and hunger. The importance of Odysseus restraining himself from temptation in order to save himself and those around him. A sacrifice of not giving in. Not being selfish. Loving others more than himself.

The clicking of heels echoed down the hall. Miles shot to his feet, closing his book. A hopeful grin spread across his face as he expected Meg to appear, but it was Alexandra who rounded the corner, her expression unreadable. It always surprised Miles how much the sisters looked alike, but how easy it was for him to tell them apart.

He sat back down, disappointed.

Her eyes flicked to the book he held in his hands. "Ah, well if it isn't our Row Bachelor," Alexandra drawled, her voice taking on that condescending tone she seemed to reserve for Miles.

"Alexandra," Miles replied, offering her a slight, polite head nod in her direction.

"Waiting for my sister, I'm assuming?" she asked, gliding over to the statue of Alecto and running her hand along its arm. The gesture seemed possessive.

"Yeah, but she should be finishing up soon." He added a silent "I hope" under his breath. "You aren't coming tonight?"

She shook her head, her eyes never leaving the statue. "No, I have some things to attend to." Then she craned her neck toward him and cocked her head once their eyes met. This was a gesture that Miles had seen Meg do many times in their last few days together. Whenever Meg did that same movement, it made her look sweet and innocent. But when Alexandra did it, she looked too much like a predator measuring its prey. "Actually, some of those things have to do with the final ceremony for Row Bachelor. It's gonna be a fun one. I assure you." She gazed up at the Alecto statue as though she were sharing this information with the inanimate Fury as opposed to Miles.

"I can't wait," was all Miles said.

Alexandra pushed herself off the statue, stalking toward Miles. She glanced around the room. "Would you like a tour of our home?"

"Oh, no. I shouldn't. I should wait here for your sister. She'll probably be done soon."

With a roll of her eyes and an exasperated sigh, Alexandra grabbed Miles by the hand and pulled him off the couch. He was thrown off guard by her strength. "Please, if I know my sister, which I do, she'll be at *least* another fifteen minutes. Plenty of time to show you around."

And with that, Alexandra dragged Miles throughout Omega Beta Mu, showing him room after room.

The kitchen was a sight to behold. If Derek had been there to see it, he would have never wanted to leave. Even with a sorority filled with girls, he'd have never guessed that they'd have three refrigerators. And not mini-fridges either. No, these were practically walk-ins. Full-sized, stainless steel behemoths. And, as if that wasn't enough, there was also a pantry the size of a small grocery store. If the boys at Alpha Xi Pi saw what their kitchen situation was like, there would be a riot on Greek Row for sure. Especially since their small, perpetually sticky kitchen housed more dust bunnies than it did actual food.

The next spot that they walked through was their personal gym. Treadmills and ellipticals in every direction. And of course it wouldn't have been complete without the bronze Greek statue that stood in the corner near the yoga mats. A plaque at the base of the statue read "Nike".

"Like the shoes?" Miles asked.

"No, Nee-keh."

Miles gave her a blank stare.

Alexandra let out a groan as if she were dealing with some impertinent child. "Yes, Miles, like the shoes." She crossed her arms. "Do you seriously not know *anything* about the mythology of the Greeks?"

"Nope. My parents have never talked about it." Miles held up his book. "But this has given me some insight."

Alexandra scoffed. "I mean, that's one interpretation."

Miles wasn't quite sure what she meant by that, but before he could ask her anything, she swept him toward another room that took his breath away.

The arcade.

There were pinball machines, racing games, and they had their very own *Ms. Pac-Man* arcade cabinet.

"You girls actually play these games?" Miles rested his hand on the glass case of a pinball machine, itching to insert a coin and play.

Alexandra trailed a sharp finger down the pinball machine, creating an annoying high-pitched scratch that rattled Miles' eardrums. Like nails on a chalkboard.

"Not really. We mainly keep this room to entertain boys." She observed the way Miles was practically drooling over the games. "Which clearly works well." She took Miles by the shoulders and steered him out of the room. Her nails dug into his shoulders like claws. "There's one last place I want to show you."

The two travelled down a spiral staircase. The steps went on forever in a dizzying corkscrew. It felt like she was leading him to a dungeon. Catacombs beneath Omega Beta Mu. When they finally reached the bottom, they were met by a narrow hallway surrounded by stone walls. Sconce lights lined the corridor, providing eerie shadow lighting. To the right, at one end of the hall, was a singular door. It was dark gray and riddled with cracks, but etched in the door frame was gold filigree that looked like ancient symbols. To the left were wooden double doors that looked fairly normal. Alexandra took them toward the left.

"What's down there?" Miles pointed to the door she was leading them away from.

Alexandra peered at him from the corner of her eyes. "There will be time for you to see what's behind door number two another day."

Miles didn't like the way she made that sound.

When they reached the double doors, Alexandra grasped the bronze handles and twisted them. They swung open and revealed a room that would be best described as a museum. Trophies were displayed in various cases around the room. Yearbooks were showcased on viewing tables, organized in chronological order. Pendants, posters, and photos were strategically hung on the walls.

"Welcome to Omega Beta Mu's history room." Alexandra waved her hands around the room with pride.

Miles absorbed the room, taking in the past of Omega Beta Mu, and while it was interesting, he didn't understand why Alexandra would think this would be the room to impress him the most. He kind of wished they were back in the arcade.

"This is cool and all, but why'd you want to show me this?" Miles asked.

Alexandra walked over to the yearbook table. She plucked one up, flipping through the pages, and handed it to him, her finger resting on one particular girl. "I thought you'd want to see your mom."

Miles set down Homer's *Odyssey* and held the yearbook, looking at the photo of his mom. She was surrounded by a bunch of other girls, but she stood out. Her smile was so bright and genuine. He memorized the photo, wondering why his mom never revealed to him that she was from Omega Beta Mu. His eyes scanned the page, where he saw another figure that looked oddly familiar. He glanced up at Alexandra, then back to the photo. The woman looked exactly like her.

Was it Alexandra?

No. That couldn't be possible because that would make her his mom's age, right? And she definitely wasn't.

Alexandra trailed the line of Miles' gaze to the photograph nestled on the page. She snapped it shut. She placed the book back on the table. Then she picked Homer's *Odyssey* up and handed it back to him. "You know what the craziest thing about Greek history is?"

Miles shrugged his shoulders.

"The fact that in almost every tale, it's the children who suffer for their parents' transgressions. And the parents never acknowledge their suffering. In most cases, they just go off and have more children. Continuing the toxic cycle over and over again." She continued, her voice soft, "And unfortunately, that's the heritage we've been given. We're a part of Greek history. Woven into its very fabric." She gracefully slinked behind Miles, wrapping her arm across his shoulders, and then she whispered in his ear. "And something you need to know about Greek history is that most of the stories end in tragedy."

Chapter Ten

Tragedy. A word that stuck with Miles the rest of the day. Clung to his skin like a spirit that wasn't ready to leave. He didn't really understand why Alexandra felt the need to tell him what she did. The veiled almost-warning she let slip. Maybe she was just messing with him. Or maybe it was a challenge because she wanted him to learn about his heritage. Either way, he used it as an opportunity to check out even more books on Greek mythology from the library. And she was right. Almost all of them ended in tragedy.

The rise and fall of heroes. The harsh punishments. The dramatic epics. The ancient sorrows.

Miles tapped his foot impatiently as he held the clear phone up to his ear, listening to the other end ring. The plastic was cool against his hot skin. He was calling home for the first time since arriving at Greek Row. He wanted to tell his mom all about his time here so far, but he also had some questions for her. Finally, there was a click, and he heard his brother's voice on the other end.

"Hello?" Jesse said, unenthusiastically, as if the last thing he wanted to do was answer the phone.

"Jess, it's Miles," he responded, trying to keep irritation from his voice.

"Miles?" Jesse sounded like he had no idea who Miles was. Pretending he was hearing that name for the first time in his entire life.

Miles pinched the bridge of his nose and groaned. "Would you put Mom on the phone?" His patience was wearing thin. It always did when it came to Jesse.

"Oh, *that* Miles." Jesse chuckled, the sound grating. "Mom!" he bellowed.

Miles pulled the phone away from his face to protect his eardrum from rupturing. If he could have reached through the phone and punched Jesse, he would have.

There was a shuffle on the other end, and then his mom's voice, warm and familiar, came through. "Hello?"

"Hey, Mom!" It was good to hear her.

"Miles." She sounded surprised, a hint of laughter in her tone. "How are you, sweetheart?"

"I'm good," he said, settling into his bean bag chair. He then proceeded to give her the rundown on Greek Row so far. Of course, he left out all the strange parts like Scylla and the dead man with the bugs. Didn't want her to worry after all. Or make her think that her son was going crazy.

"Well, that sounds wonderful, dear." There was something distant in her voice, though. Distracted. It bothered Miles. But her distracted tone made it easier for him to ask her about the secrets she'd been keeping.

"Mom, I really called to ask you something." Miles cleared his throat, the words feeling thick on his tongue as he finally asked, "Why didn't you ever tell me that you were in Omega Beta Mu?"

Silence. It stretched between the two landlines. More silence.

Finally, she spoke, a bit reluctant-sounding. "Miles, I don't see how any of that is important. It was so long ago. A lifetime almost, really. And honestly, I don't remember much about it. A blur. There was so much going on in college, you know, with classes and friends, and then meeting your father and—"

"Yeah, I know all that," Miles interrupted, not wanting her to go off on a tangent about their love story that he'd already heard a million times before. "It's just …"

"What, Miles?" Her voice sounded flat, devoid of the warmth it usually held.

"It sucks to hear about your past from other people. I feel like I don't know anything about you or Dad or even my heritage. Like there's a whole side of my family that's been hidden. But then, everyone else here seems to know all about the Pappases. And I feel like an idiot because I don't know anything about it. Not you or Dad or the Greeks."

"And who is this *everyone* you speak of?" Now she seemed demanding. Her question was sharp, and it was very out of character for his mom to sound anything other than sickeningly sweet.

Miles was going to try to appeal to her normal, sweet nature again. "Her name is Alexandra Cronos. She's the president of Omega Beta Mu. Well, she and her sister are the president. Oh, man, Mom, her sister is amazing. Meghan. You'd love her." He was ready to spiral into telling her how much he liked Meghan, thinking it would make her think about her love story with his dad. Maybe that would get her back to normal.

But before he could continue, she cut in. "What exactly has she told you?"

"Do you know them?" Miles remembered the photo of the girl he'd seen who looked so much like Alexandra. He could only assume that his mom knew their relatives. Maybe there was some sort of forgotten family drama—something that Miles wouldn't know anything about—that stemmed from there.

"Miles—I ... you really need to focus on your studies. Ignore the girls." The command hung in the air for a moment.

"It's a little late for that, Mom. Hard to avoid the girls when I'm Row Bachelor." He didn't mention that earlier because Row Bachelor was supposed to be one of those unspoken rituals on Greek Row, but, considering his mom used to attend here, he figured there was no harm in telling her now.

Again, silence stretched between them. Then, "I have to go, Miles. Jesse has soccer practice." The excuse felt flimsy, especially since Jesse hated playing sports. Miles didn't even know he was on the soccer team.

"Mom—" Miles started, desperate for her to stay on the phone. To unravel some bit of history that she seemed to push away.

But there was a click, sharp and final, and the line went dead, leaving Miles alone with the sound of disconnected beeping and a swirling vortex of unanswered questions.

"Come on, Miles. You've been sucked into those books for hours now. Let's goooooo." Phinn whined, spinning his basketball on his finger.

"I know, I know. I've just fallen down the Greek rabbit hole." Miles reluctantly placed *Mythology* by Edith Hamilton down on his small desk. He had picked up the books from the library after his phone call with his mom. If she wasn't going to tell him anything, he could at least take matters into his own hands and read about the stories and myths that shaped the Greeks. It gave him a sense of the beliefs of his people.

Derek brushed chip crumbs off his shirt and sprawled across Miles' bed. "You're taking this Greek thing to the next level."

"Well, I am a Pappas." He tied his basketball shoes with a hard tug.

"Yeah, Derek. Cut him some slack. He's one of the few people on campus who's actually Greek." Phinn passed Miles the ball. He caught it, the worn leather rough against his hands, and dribbled it down the hall until they reached the stairs.

The three boys were going to play a game of basketball at the outdoor court on campus. Tomorrow was going to be the ceremony night for the Row Bachelor. Miles had heard whispers about the event all around campus. Stares would usually follow him as people spoke. The whole thing was hush hush, and everyone was doing their best to make sure he didn't have any idea what was going to happen.

Meg let him know that the girls at Omega Beta Mu would be too busy setting up for the event, laser-focused on what to have catered for dinner and seating charts, so they wouldn't be planning anything special tonight. Which meant he was free to just have a guys' night out.

"Neither of you are Greek?" Miles asked.

"Nope," they said at the same time.

"I didn't have the privilege of being a legacy," Phinn added.

"Same here," Derek said. "And it's costing my parents a fortune."

Phinn nodded his head. "Oh, yeah, my parents really tried to talk me out of coming to school here. They hadn't quite saved enough tuition money for me. But I promised to get a summer job to help if I could come here. They agreed in the end, although I could definitely tell they still weren't thrilled."

Miles absorbed what they told him, feeling bad that going to school here was a huge sacrifice for their families, especially when Miles knew that he'd been awarded a full ride. A ride that had nothing to do with his grades or achievements in high school—because neither would have gotten him there—but simply because he was a Pappas. Which meant something to the people on Greek Row, but nothing to Miles because he had no idea what being a Pappas even meant.

The basketball court was completely empty. Humidity created a thickness in the air, causing sweat to already form on Miles' brow. He glanced up at the sky and saw the dark clouds rolling in, an explanation as to why everyone seemed to be indoors. Lightning lit up the grey skies in the distance. A couple of fat raindrops landed on Miles' head.

"You guys sure you wanna play? It looks like a storm is brewing?" Miles shook the droplets from his hair.

Phinn glanced up at the clouds and smiled. "Heck yeah. This will be perfect."

"Alright, are we playing Pig or? ..." Miles dribbled the ball as he waited for their response.

"Let's do a three-point shootout," Phinn suggested.

"Ooh, yeah, the better our three-pointers are, the more the girls will be impressed and the guys will be jealous." Derek stole the ball right out from underneath Miles' hands and went up to the three-point line. He lined up his shot, bent his knees, did a slight jump, and, with a flick of the wrist, released the ball. It zoomed through the air. Miles held his breath as he watched the orange sphere make it to the hoop. It circled the rim but ended up rolling away from the net, bouncing onto the ground below.

Miles released his breath, chuckling at Derek's failed attempt. "That counts as your first shot."

Derek chased the ball. "Oh, come on! We didn't start yet. That was a practice shot."

"Nope," Phinn joined in. "That was your first shot. You get four more."

Derek groaned in reply, but he didn't argue. Instead, he went in for his second shot. The boys played like that for a while. Each taking turns doing five shots to see who could get the most three-pointers.

Miles was impressed by his first shot. It was nothing but net, creating a satisfying *swoosh* as it went in. He'd like to say it was because he was good at the sport, but in reality, he knew it was just beginner's luck.

Phinn won the first, second, and third rounds, which wasn't much of a surprise. The guy was an amazing shooter. Miles was shocked that he hadn't made it on the basketball team at the university.

Phinn went to the left corner pocket for his next shot. Thunder rumbled. Miles looked up to see that the sky had gotten even darker, almost black.

"Guys, I think we should call it quits. It looks like it's gonna get bad." Miles didn't want to be caught in a torrential downpour.

"I just have two more shots! I can beat the storm." Phinn was determined to sweep the boys in another round.

More thunder. Closer.

Lightning flashed, illuminating the basketball court.

"Hurry up, Phinn," Derek urged. Miles assumed that Derek only wanted to rush Phinn to mess him up. After all, if Phinn missed one of his shots, it would mean Derek won this round.

"Shut up, Derek. You're making me lose my focus."

Another roll of thunder. Miles glanced up to see the next flash of lightning. The sky lit up, and from behind one of the clouds, the flash revealed a silhouette. Miles squinted at the outline of what appeared to be a large winged creature. The sky went dark again. Maybe he was just seeing things. He shook his head, trying to clear his vision and mind.

A screech echoed from above, resounding over the clash of thunder. Miles jerked his head upward again. The winged creature radiated in the storm. This time closer. Swooping down beneath the clouds now. It was gaining speed and travelling toward the basketball court.

"Uh, guys." Miles' voice sounded small as he pointed to the figure. "What's that?"

The boys looked up. Miles could hear the drop of the basketball on the court. The ball rolled across the ground, and he felt it bump into his foot. Taking a brave moment, he took his eyes off the winged creature to see the reactions of Phinn and Derek. He wanted to make sure they were seeing what he was seeing. He needed to know that he wasn't imagining things.

From the dropped jaws of his two friends, Miles knew that they were all witnessing the same thing flapping in the sky.

There was a clap of thunder, and then another. The thunder began to take on a familiar rhythm. A specific chant that Miles had recently come to know.

"*Thysia. Thysia. Thysia,*" the thunder seemed to say. "*Thysia. Thysia. Thysia.*"

Miles tracked the creature again with his eyes. It was the seconds when the sky went dark, when they would lose sight of the flying figure, that made Miles' heart thump the most.

Lightning flash.

The creature shrieked.

Lightning flash.

OMEGA BETA MONSTER

It flapped its wings.

Lightning flash.

It hovered above the basketball court.

Lightning flash.

The creature dove. Right for the boys.

Chapter Eleven

"Run for your life!" Miles roared, his voice battling the thunder, awakening the rain that the clouds had been holding onto. He didn't take the time to see if Phinn and Derek listened to his command and followed him, but he could hear the sound of their tennis shoes slapping against the pavement, splashing through puddles right behind him.

Phinn, being a natural athlete, was faster than Miles and Derek. He took the lead, passing by Miles like a track star. But despite Miles' lack of athleticism, he continued to run as fast as he could. The rain was now creating a relentless assault as the raindrops pelted his eyes, threatening to blind him.

The world narrowed to just the space in front of him. A blurred canvas of rain and shadows. His chest burned like a furnace. Aching and painful. He pumped his legs as hard as he could. Desperate to stay ahead of the creature. His sides screamed at him to take a second to breathe. His muscles had already felt weak and tired from the hours of playing basketball. They trembled and wobbled as he ran, but he refused to stop.

Well, at least that was until he heard Derek's cry slice through the storm, shattering Miles' pace as it resounded from somewhere behind him.

Miles spun, gasping for air, to see Derek sprawled on the ground, cradling his ankle with a grimace of pain. With a quick, panicked glance at the sky, Miles saw the winged creature plummeting straight for Derek. He wouldn't leave his friend behind.

Fueled by fear and adrenaline, his exhaustion long forgotten, Miles raced to Derek's side, but the creature reached him first, and as Miles approached even closer, he could make out its appearance.

It had the features of a crone, etched with centuries of horror, with feathered wings that spread far and wide. Its long white hair blew in the wind and rain. Pale snakes with bright red eyes coiled themselves in its hair.

It screeched, sharp fangs gleaming as it reached out its taloned feet to claw at Derek's shoulders, attempting to grasp him.

Miles' eyes widened in shock, his breath hitching in his throat. He knew that face. Knew the wings that were beating against the wind with unnatural force, the stringy, ethereal hair billowing behind it. And that face. A face that struck him the first day he saw it. This was Alecto. The statue that resided in the foyer of the Omega Beta Mu mansion.

But how could that be possible? Statues don't come alive. They don't make a sound, or fly, and they definitely don't try to tear you and your friends apart with razor-like talons. And yet, here was one, Alecto, alive, breathing, and terrifying. Trying to attack Miles and his friends. Attempting to carry Derek off into the storm.

Miles watched with paralyzing dread as Derek struggled against Alecto. Her talons buried into his shoulder like grappling hooks, and he cried out.

Derek spotted Miles through the storm. "Miles, run! Save yourself!"

Miles could hear the crack of pain and terror in Derek's voice. There was no way he would abandon him. Miles was determined to save his friend from this beast.

His eyes darted around, searching through the darkness and rain to find anything that could help him. Finally, he saw that the storm had knocked a branch off one of the nearby trees. He took the branch, dragging it behind him, to Derek and Alecto. When he reached them, with all his strength, he hoisted the branch up, brandishing it like a baseball bat, and swung at Alecto with a guttural yell.

WHACK!

The branch connected, hitting Alecto right in her crone-like face with a sickening thud, leaving behind three bright red scratches, fiery welts, across her cheek. A high-pitched shriek of pure fury tore from her lips. The noise seemed to amplify the storm itself, setting off bolts of lightning in every direction.

Her claws released Derek as she recoiled, and she floated up further above them, cradling her cheek. With Alecto now distracted by her wound, Miles seized the opportunity to pick Derek up off the muddy ground. Derek's ankle was clearly injured, most likely sprained. Miles swung his arm around Derek and let him lean his weight on him as the two hobbled across the lawn.

Derek whimpered in pain at every movement, but there was no time for them to hesitate. Not with Alecto still hanging around. Who knew how long she would be distracted for? Safety. They needed to get to safety, but where?

Miles frantically searched, panic gnawing at him as he felt like the clock was ticking against them, and then he heard Phinn's voice call out, cutting through the wind.

"Guys, over here! Get to the trees!" Phinn shouted. He was standing at the treeline of the woods that bordered the school's campus, his figure vivid against the foliage with his bright yellow jersey.

The perfect sanctuary. A natural defense. If they could make it to the woods, Alecto wouldn't be able to penetrate the dense canopy with her massive wings.

Miles and Derek sprinted as fast as Derek's injured ankle would allow so they could get to the trees. Miles' heart hammered in his chest when he heard the unmistakable screech of Alecto from behind them. He cursed under his breath. He had hoped the blow from the branch would have left her stunned a little bit longer. But she had recomposed herself and was now after them with renewed wrath.

He glimpsed back, his blood turning to ice when he saw that she was quickly gaining on them. Hatred burned in her eyes as her face twisted into a grotesque scowl, pushing her wings even harder, closing the distance between them.

Miles strained, trying to go faster, but with the added weight of Derek, it was becoming difficult. Each step was more and more of an effort. And now Derek's breathing was becoming ragged. Miles glanced at him, seeing that Derek's face was pale, but his cheeks were flushed. Derek was in a lot of pain, and Miles couldn't make him go any faster because of it.

Miles' heart sank into the pit of his stomach. The truth was a bitter pill to swallow. There was no way they were going to make it to the trees in time. And who knew what Alecto would do when she reached them again. Miles could almost feel her talons digging into him. Piercing his skin like knives.

Then, Miles saw Phinn leave the protection of the woods and run toward them. He slipped beneath Derek's other arm, and together the trio raced to the trees.

When they were about five feet away, they dove, sliding across the mud and foliage to reach the safety of the woods.

Miles rolled over onto his back, his gaze fixed on the sky. Alecto made it to the woods and stopped, hovering in the air above them. Miles was right; Alecto wasn't able to get through the trees. He gave her the finger, and she let out a frustrated scream of rage, glaring directly at Miles with her pale eyes. He smirked at her in triumph.

Like a bat out of Hell, Alecto whipped around, her massive wings beating in the air with unadulterated power, and flew up into the dark, swirling storm clouds, the sound of her wings fading as she disappeared.

Chapter Twelve

"What was *that?!*" Phinn panted, slamming the door to the Alpha Xi Pi house behind them and locking it.

Miles' heart was still pounding in his chest. He was relieved to at least be in the safety of their fraternity. "That was Alecto." Blank stares met him. "You know. Ancient Greece. Mythological being. Fury?"

"I mean, it definitely *was* furious." Derek slid to the floor, still cradling his ankle. "Do you think we should call 911? Maybe we should call 911."

Miles rolled his eyes. "No. *It* was a *Fury*. And tell 911 what, exactly? They'll never believe us. We'll end up getting blamed for something else. I guarantee it.

They'll say we're either doing drugs or drinking or that it's some hazing ritual."

"And what exactly is a Fury, Miles?" Phinn asked.

"If not 911, shouldn't we get some sort of help? There has to be someone on campus who would believe us, right?" Derek whined. The boys were all frantically talking over one another.

Miles couldn't take the jumble of words anymore. He held up a finger and then rushed up the staircase to their room. A stack of mythology books rested on the stand next to his bed. He grabbed one from the middle of the pile, knocking the rest of the stack onto the floor, and ran back down the stairs.

Flipping to the table of contents, Miles scanned for the page that discussed the Furies, also known as Erinyes, according to Meg. Page 92.

"Furies, or Erinyes, were deities of vengeance. They punished wrongdoing and served justice for crimes such as murder, perjury, and betrayal. They embodied the idea that actions have consequences. They were three sisters, Alecto, Megeara, and Tisiphone. Their purpose for justice was born out of a story of family betrayal, one theme common in many Greek tales." Miles slammed the book shut, giving his friends a grave look.

"And you think that's what attacked us?" Phinn's voice was one of disbelief.

"Do you have any other suggestions as to what it could have been? Please, I'm all ears."

Silence followed.

Derek shimmied up from the floor. He winced a few times in the process. "This is crazy. Greek mythology is just that; mythology."

"Says the man with the scratches on his shoulder from Fury talons." Miles pointed to Derek's torn shirt. Blood dripped down the front, already starting to turn dark red as it clotted.

Derek glanced at the open scratches. His eyes glazed over, and his legs became unsteady at the sight. Miles and Phinn reacted with cat-like instincts as they grabbed him by the arms before he could faint.

Derek vigorously shook his head. "Thanks, guys. I'm okay."

"So, why did that ... Fury ... attack us?" Phinn asked. They started working their way toward the stairs.

Miles thought hard. Since he'd gotten here, mythological monsters had been targeting him left and right, but he had no idea why. And then the odd circumstances surrounding how he'd been chosen as Row

Bachelor were also a mystery. Even though he had no idea why, it was clear that these things were connected and that Fury was out to get him. His friends were poor bystanders caught in the mix.

But Miles was too scared to voice his thoughts out loud. To tell his friends that *he* was somehow the cause for the attack. Even though he rationally knew it wasn't his fault, something inside of him made it feel as though it was. Fear of losing the people he'd grown closest to in the last few days made him clamp down on his tongue. If they knew what Miles was thinking, they might avoid him like the plague. It could spread to the rest of campus, to Meg, and no one would want anything to do with Miles.

Instead of telling them the truth, all Miles said was, "I don't know, but we definitely aren't gonna be able to sleep tonight."

Derek let out a yawn. "Yeah, right! I'm exhausted. My adrenaline left a while ago, and my blood sugar is screaming at me."

"Okay, fine. We work in shifts. I'll take the first watch while you guys sleep." Miles grabbed one of Phinn's baseball bats sitting in the corner of the room. He placed a bean bag chair in front of the bedroom door and plopped down.

"Should we tell the other guys in the house?" Derek asked.

"They'll only think we're crazy," Miles said.

"You really think that thing will come back for us?" Phinn asked, helping Derek into bed.

"No idea."

Knock. Knock. Knock.

The front door.

The boys jumped and went on high alert.

Miles and Phinn slowly tiptoed to the top of the stairs, leaving the injured Derek behind.

Knock. Knock. Knock.

The door handle jiggled.

"You wait here. If anything happens, get help," Miles whispered to Phinn, who nodded in return.

With tentative steps, Miles descended toward what could possibly be his impending doom. It seemed silly to believe that a Fury that openly attacked them in a field would then nonchalantly knock at their front door, but Miles wasn't taking any chances. At this point, he would believe that Hades himself was on the other side of that door, ready to drag him down to the Underworld.

Knock.

Miles turned the lock.

Knock.

He twisted the doorknob.

Knock.

He swung the door open and brandished his weapon.

Meg screamed at the sight. "Miles?! What are you doing?"

"Meg? What are you doing?" they said at the same time.

"I brought you guys some chocolate chip cookies. Special recipe. Homemade." With shaky hands, Meg held out a plate of cookies wrapped in cellophane and tied with a fancy red ribbon. "I felt bad about not being able to do much for you today because of preparations for tomorrow, so I figured this would suffice." She pulled the plate close to her body, and then she asked, "So, what's with the baseball bat?"

Miles almost forgot that he was even holding the bat. He was still surprised to see that it was Meg standing at the door and not another being ripped from the pages of a Greek textbook. He put the weapon next to the door and ushered Meg inside. Before he closed the door, Miles took one last glance at the sky, wondering if he'd catch a glimpse of Alecto circling their house.

The skies were empty.

"I didn't mean to scare you like that. I thought you were someone else." *Something else.*

Meg bit her lip. "And you were going to beat this person with a baseball bat? Did they do something to you? Should I call campus security?"

"No!"

Meg looked taken aback.

"Sorry. It's just ..."

Meg placed a reassuring hand on Miles' arm. "It's okay, Miles. You can tell me."

Miles' eyes darted around the room. He felt as though someone could be listening in on this conversation. He dropped his voice low. "Have you ever experienced anything *odd* on campus? Seen anything strange?"

Meg pursed her lips in thought. "One time, a frat boy released a bunch of live chickens on campus. That was a little strange."

Miles let out an exasperated breath. "Not like that." Time for a moment of vulnerability and truth. "I've been seeing these ... monsters ... everywhere. Things like Scylla from the Odyssey and Alecto."

"You mean like the Alecto statue at Omega Beta Mu?"

"Except it wasn't a statue. It was the real deal."

Footsteps rushed down the stairs. "Miles, you okay?" Phinn's voice wavered.

"I'm fine. It was just Meg at the door. She brought cookies."

Meg held out the cookies to Phinn.

"Did I hear cookies?!" Derek's voice shouted from the bedroom upstairs. It figured that Derek would be able to pick out the word "cookies" and not anything else.

"Phinn and Derek saw Alecto, too. Tell her."

Phinn started in on the entire terrifying experience, starting at the beginning of the thunderstorm.

Meg nodded her head the whole time. Miles couldn't tell if she was trying to appease them by listening or if she truly believed them. When Phinn finished his version of the story, Meg released a breath. "It sounds like you guys have had a rough night."

"You believe us?" Miles was hopeful.

"I believe that you guys believe what you experienced, and I'm not going to downplay your experience or feed into it because I simply was not there."

Miles thought she was acting too chill. Like she'd heard this type of story before, but wasn't admitting to it.

She moved to untie the ribbon around the plate of cookies, opening up the cellophane. The smell of chocolatey baked goods wafted into the air. "What I do know is that you all sound like you need some delicious cookies in your life to take the edge off."

The smell was so enticing. Miles' stomach rumbled. They looked fresh. Ooey gooey. As if Meg had just pulled them out of the oven.

Phinn didn't need any convincing. He reached for three cookies, shoving them all into his mouth. Stress eating at its finest.

And even though Miles wanted to copy the movement, there was something wriggling in the back of his mind telling him that eating cookies wasn't going to solve his monster problem.

He went to voice this to Meg. Tell her that he appreciated the gesture, but he couldn't bring himself to eat the cookie when there was so much chaos going on in his world. But it was like she knew *exactly* what he was about to say.

She pressed a manicured finger up to his lips. Leaning in closely, she whispered to him, her words curling around him like a siren's song. *"Just one bite, Miles."* And then she held a cookie to his mouth.

Miles took a bite, letting an explosion of flavor dance across his tongue. He thoroughly chewed and chewed. It wasn't until the cookie hit the back of his throat that a bitter aftertaste coated his tongue.

"Isn't it *so* yummy?" Meg asked.

"Delicious," Phinn said, garbling from the chewing.

Miles gulped the rest of his bite down. "Yeah, real good. You said it was a special recipe?"

"Yep! An ancient one. Made with a surprising secret ingredient." She smiled brightly.

"What's the secret? I promise not to tell." Miles delivered a coy smile.

"Pinky swear?" Meg asked, holding out her pinky to him. Miles' heart flipped around and then righted itself as he wrapped his pinky around hers.

"Lotus oil. It'll help ease all of your anxieties." She winked. "Anyway, I better get going. Make sure to share some cookies with Derek, please!"

"Yeah! Don't eat all the cookies!" Derek called down.

Chapter Thirteen

After Meg left, things got better but weirder. Derek and Phinn couldn't stop eating the chocolate chip cookies. Miles took a couple more bites of his, feeling more relaxed as he did, like he was walking amongst the clouds, but he couldn't bring himself to finish it. The aftertaste was getting to him.

Derek and Phinn, however, became two laughing goofballs as they chomped away. Everything was funny to them. They started making jokes about the Alecto situation, and it was really starting to grate on Miles' nerves.

"What's a Fury's favorite game?" Derek started.

"What?" Phinn chuckled.

"Truth or vengeance!" The two boys cracked up. Miles didn't find any of it funny.

Eventually, to Miles' relief, the two boys fell sound asleep.

Miles sat watch at the entrance to their bedroom. His friends might be able to turn the night into a joke, but he couldn't.

Before he knew it, though, Miles' eyes were also growing heavy. He tossed and turned all night long, fighting the urge to sleep, perspiring through his pajamas with a cold sweat. Every time his eyes started to close, he would see Alecto, swooping down to take him away. Her leathery wings wrapping around his body to suffocate him. The sound of her screech replaying like a broken cassette tape in his ears. And then his eyes would shoot back open.

His mind raced with thoughts of how weird his life had gotten in the short week he had been on Greek Row. It was like the pathway to Greek Row led straight through an invisible portal to the Underworld, and somehow, he was a trigger for all beasts that resided there.

It wasn't just his safety at risk anymore. Now his friends were involved. Maybe Meg would be next. He couldn't risk the lives of those he cared about. The more he thought about it, the more he realized he needed to get out of here, the Row Bachelor ceremony be damned.

With his mind made up, Miles grabbed two empty duffel bags that rested on the floor underneath his bed. He reached for them, unzipped them, and began to load up the life he'd brought to Greek Row with him.

He started with his clothes, going through his drawers and closet in a frenzy, pulling out shirts and pants. Forget folding. Forget neatness. No, that would take too much time. He crammed the clothes into the bag. A jumbled mess of fabric. He'd worry about ironing them when he was safe at home again.

Next were his electronics and books. These items he packed with care, still trying to keep up the pace, but realizing that if he ruined any of these items, his parents would most likely not replace them for his carelessness.

Miles was so stuck in his own little world of bustling around to get the heck out of Alpha Xi Pi that he didn't realize how much noise he was making. Clothes rustling, drawers slamming, and the zipping and unzipping of duffel bags. It wasn't until he heard Phinn groan that he became aware of the fact that he was being loud.

"Dude, what's with the early wake up call? It's Saturday," Phinn mumbled, his voice thick with sleep. He rubbed his eyes. His face was crinkled in a combination of confusion and annoyance.

Miles looked out the window. The sun had barely risen. He didn't notice how early it was when he started. He was running on adrenaline and the need to leave.

"Yeah, man, it's only six," Derek chimed in. He pushed himself up in his bed, and his hair stuck out in all sorts of crazy directions.

"Sorry, guys. I guess I didn't realize the time," Miles apologized and finally took a moment to catch his breath. He sank down onto the edge of his now-bare mattress. "I need to get out of here, though. Now."

Phinn swung his legs out from beneath his *Lion King* comforter set. Miles and Derek had teased him relentlessly for the blanket when they first saw it, but deep down, Miles loved *The Lion King*, too. "What? But tonight is the Row Bachelor ceremony! You can't leave now."

Miles almost choked on his spit, completely stunned that Phinn didn't understand why he'd be so eager to leave. After the terrifying fiasco last night, Miles would have thought they'd all be up and packing today. "Um, you guys are still cool staying here after we almost got ripped apart by that flying beast last night?"

"What flying beast?" Derek genuinely asked, pushing past a yawn and brushing cookie crumbs off his chest. The empty plate was resting between Derek's bed and Phinn's.

"You're joking, right?" Miles asked. He was met with silence from Phinn and Derek as the two looked at each other and then back to Miles. "We were attacked on the basketball court, running for our lives in the middle of the storm?" Miles was exasperated at the fact that he was wasting time and energy retelling them the events that took place last night. But judging from their dumbfounded expressions, Miles believed they had no idea what he was talking about. "You guys seriously don't remember?"

"I think I would remember if some wild, flying monster attacked us." Phinn switched on the TV, turning the channel so he could watch *Saved by the Bell: The New Class*.

Miles took the remote from Phinn's hand and shut it off. This was no time for them to get distracted. Miles needed answers. He stomped over to Derek's bed and ripped off his covers. He scanned Derek's body for a sprained ankle, but there was no sign of injury.

"Hey!" Derek shouted in annoyance.

"What about your shoulder?" Miles asked, pointing to Derek's shoulder that Alecto had clenched in her raptor claw.

Derek slipped his shirt off. A blank canvas. No marks on his body.

No. There was no way that Miles was remembering the turn of events incorrectly. He could maybe pass off Scylla and Char as figments of his imagination. *Maybe*. But this? No. Last night, his friends were just as terrified as he was of the Fury that came barrelling from the skies in a—well, fury. And then Meg showed up with the cookies and–

The cookies.

That had to be the only logical explanation. There was something in those cookies that made his friends forget. Something that healed their wounds ...

What'd Meg say the secret ingredient was?

Miles racked his brain trying to think, but even some parts of his memory were foggy. He glanced at the floor and saw his own half-eaten cookie resting there. He stomped on it with his foot, turning it to cookie dust.

"I'm leaving." His mind was made up. It was clear that things on Greek Row were not safe for him anymore. It appeared that even Meg, someone he thought he could trust, was a part of this somehow.

"Whoa, whoa, whoa," Phinn started. "You can't leave!"

"Yeah, man. You'd be giving all this—" Derek waved his hands around. "—up. And your parents would be so disappointed. You're here on a *free* ride."

"Not only that, but tonight is the Row Bachelor ceremony. Think of how upset Meg would be if you missed it."

"You just don't get it." Miles threw himself down on a bean bag chair with a sigh. "Ever since I got here, I feel like I've been losing my mind. It's like I've got some kind of Greek curse attached to me, and I can't seem to catch a break."

Derek clapped a hand on his shoulder. "Miles, my man, I get it. We're all going through some really weird changes right now. This ain't high school anymore. This is the big leagues, and the stress is getting to all of us in different ways."

"What Derek said. You're probably just homesick, and your brain is trying to create these imaginative monsters to give you an excuse to leave. To go back to mommy and daddy."

"I'm not homesick. This is something else entirely."

"Okay fine. Let's say it is something else. Don't you want to get to the bottom of it? Get your answers? And I bet the perfect place to find those answers would be at the Row Bachelor ceremony." Phinn knelt down next to Miles, meeting him eye to eye.

Miles thought about what his friends were saying. He did need answers. Either this was some really sick prank that was being played on him, or the gods were truly out to torture him.

One more night on Greek Row. Get his answers. See the Row Bachelor ceremony all the way through and end these Greek horrors once and for all.

Chapter Fourteen

Twinkling lights lit up the path all the way to the Omega Beta Mu mansion. Streamers hung from the branches of trees. Tiki torches burned in the distance. The full moon hung in the sky. Meg laced her arm through Miles' and rested her head on his shoulder as they strolled toward the mansion.

The moment Meg showed up at the doorstep of Alpha Xi Pi wearing a flowing purple dress, her head adorned by a laurel crown that looked as though it were pure gold next to her pale hair, Miles could barely even remember his own name, let alone anything about monsters. Her presence alone was like some magical spell.

He was actually starting to hate the way she made him feel because it made it that much harder to demand answers. To accuse her of giving him laced cookies. Blame her for the monsters running through his mind.

"You look beautiful, by the way," Miles' voice came out all breathy and awkward, but he wasn't embarrassed by it when he saw the way that Meg blushed.

"Well, tonight is a special event." Meg glanced up at the night sky. "And look at how gorgeous that moon is. The gods are truly smiling down on us."

"So, you believe in all the gods stuff? The Greek mythology?" Miles asked.

Meg giggled in return. "Of course I do. It's part of our history."

"So when I told you about Alecto, you believed that, right?"

"Would it make you feel better if I told you yes?" Meg asked, quirking a blonde eyebrow.

Miles shrugged. "I don't know. It would make me feel less crazy. None of this started happening to me until I got here. Until I met you and became Row Bachelor."

"So you're blaming me?" Meg's voice had darkened.

"Should I?"

"Look, I'm not going to lull you into a sense of security. This place is rich with history. The blood of gods runs through this soil. I wouldn't be surprised if you've seen ghosts of the past."

Miles audibly gulped. "You think this place is haunted?"

Meg looked up at him through pale lashes. "I think that Alexandra will explain everything to you tonight, and then you'll feel so much better."

They walked up the stairs to the mansion, and Meg stepped behind Miles when they reached the door, throwing her hands over his eyes. "No peeking," she whispered in his ear, sending a chill down his spine. There was a click from the door as it opened, and she carefully shuffled Miles inside the threshold.

Unveiling his eyes, Miles was greeted by a fully decorated foyer, full of balloons, streamers, lights, and banners that read "152nd Row Bachelor."

The girls of Omega Beta Mu were standing all around the foyer, their white-toothed grins making them appear proud. They clearly put a lot of hard work into making this night special. Miles didn't know what to say to thank them, but he gave them a sheepish grin and a wave.

As his eyes danced around the room, he noticed that one familiar face was missing from the bunch. Alexandra was nowhere in sight. Interesting since she was the other half of the president. He'd assumed she'd be the one greeting him at the door.

Another banner that hung above the entryway to the dining hall made Miles' stomach flip. This one, painted in red, said "*Thysía. Thysía. Thysía. Thysía.*"

He nudged Meg with his elbow. "What does that banner mean?"

She peered over to the banner he was pointing to. "It's a Greek saying."

"What's the saying?" he asked, nervous as to what her response might be.

"Oh, nothing. It's just a silly Row Bachelor tradition."

Miles didn't care for her response. It was too flippant. "I think I've heard—" A large arm wrapped around Miles' torso, startling him. He jumped in the air and spun around, only to be greeted by his two roommates.

"Congratulations, roomie," Derek said, already passing by Miles and toward the dining hall. Most likely headed in the direction of where the food would be.

Phinn smiled. Dressed similarly to Miles, with a white button-up shirt and black pants, Phinn opted to keep his Jordans on instead of wearing dress shoes like Miles. "Glad to see you're still here."

"Wouldn't have missed it," Miles said, although his voice didn't sound too convincing.

Meg steered the two boys to the dining hall, where they were greeted with a lavish meal. The grand wooden table spanned the length of the room. It was covered in an ornate deep blue tablecloth with gold tassels that hung off the edges. Gold coins were scattered across the table. Tall candelabras rested in the center, lit with candles that cast a warm glow throughout the room. Garlands of ivy and laurel were woven through the center of the table and around plates of food. Bowls of fresh grapes, figs, and pomegranates provided a burst of color.

The Omega Beta Mu girls, as well as a bunch of other people on campus, including his Alpha Xi Pi brothers, were seated around the table.

The smell of grilled salmon with a hint of zesty lemon filled the air. Miles' stomach gurgled in response.

Meg pulled out the chair that was at the head of the table. "Bachelor," she said as she motioned for Miles to sit down. "Can I get you a plate of food?" She asked.

After Meg's cookies last night, he was skeptical. But when he saw others filling their plates, his nerves calmed. His stomach growled. "Guess I'm hungrier than I thought I was. Of course. It all looks delicious." He handed Meg his plate, and she filled it to the brim with everything, topping it off with a huge slice of baklava.

Picking up his fork, Miles dug into the salmon. It was cooked perfectly. Cut like butter. Almost melted in his mouth as a rush of flavor danced across his tongue. Next, he tossed in some beautiful purple grapes, reveling in the way they burst in his mouth. The food was to die for.

"Welcome, everyone." The click clack of high heels made Miles' food stick in his throat.

He recognized that voice.

Alexandra.

Peering from her periphery, Alexandra sauntered toward the other end of the table. The head of the table across from Miles. "I'm glad you could all make it this evening to celebrate our 152nd Row Bachelor, Miles

Pappas." Everyone clapped, making Miles feel mildly uncomfortable as he attempted to swallow his overly chewed food. "One of the greatest Greek traditions that we can uphold is giving back to the gods. After all, who would we be, where would we be without them?" The rhetorical question hung in the air.

Miles started to feel sweat drip down his back. The room became suddenly chilly and hot all at the same time.

"And while I know that not all of you here come from the same Grecian background, on Greek Row, everyone serves the gods. We're all Greek here."

Things began to swirl and tilt in Miles' vision. With shaky hands, he dropped his fork, the clang striking his ears as it hit the side of his plate like the toll of a church bell.

"And I'm so glad to have you all a part of this sacred tradition, one that ensures our good standing with those we obey. In return, they've promised all of you success in your time on campus as well as your future endeavors. But remember not to tell of the tradition or their vow to you shall be broken and their wrath will be *endless*." Alexandra had her back to them, staring out the large bay window that looked out into the night sky.

Everyone around the table, except for Derek and Phinn, nodded their heads in solidarity while Miles struggled to even keep his head up.

What was happening to him? He felt like everything was closing in. Like his world was spinning on an axis.

That's when he noticed all the plates still piled with food. Not a single morsel touched by anyone else.

Miles had been poisoned.

Or, at the very least, drugged. Again.

He couldn't help but think about how much of an idiot he was.

The chair he sat on slipped out from under him as he crashed to the floor. Using his unsteady hands and feet, he crawled across the floor, trying to make it to the exit.

Ginormous legs like tree trunks blocked his path. Blank golden eyes burned into Miles as he peered at the living figure of Typhon, a sword shaped like a lightning bolt in his hand. And just like his dad had said, numerous snakes hissed at Miles from atop Typhon's shoulders, breathing fire in his direction.

Miles scrambled backward. Legs bumped into his back. Two pairs of lavender eyes glared down at him.

Alexandra and Meg. He couldn't believe it. Whiplash almost made him pass out when he violently shook his head back and forth. Trying to erase the image of Meg. But it didn't disappear. Meg's once gorgeous appearance was now riddled with wrinkles and a scowl. Claws were sharpened at her side. Leathery wings spread out of her back.

Miles turned his head toward her sister.

Alexandra looked like an old crone. Wings spanned behind her. Wings that looked so familiar.

Then he saw it.

The large mark on the left side of her cheek. In the spot that Miles had hit last night with a tree branch.

Alexandra was Alecto.

Chapter Fifteen

With heavy eyelids, Miles started to blink himself awake. The room around him was dim. Things slowly swam into blurry focus. The room was still slightly spinning, and he was trying to do his best to keep his food from dinner down. He swallowed hard, fighting against the urge to puke up the bile sitting in his stomach.

Torches flickered along the stone walls. It was a large chamber that looked ancient. Typhon stood guard at the door, his lightning bolt sword in his grip. Figures dressed in brown cloaks stood at attention, dark hoods covering their faces. They hummed a chant. Soft at first, but then it became more rhythmic, urgent. Mumbling hums turned into words.

"*Thysía. Thysía. Thysía. Thysía.*"

The words started to take shape in Miles' ears. What was once a jumble of gibberish to him suddenly became clear.

"*Sacrifice. Sacrifice. Sacrifice. Sacrifice.*"

No longer able to hold it down, Miles turned his head to the side and threw up.

After emptying his stomach, he did the next thing that made sense and tried to move. Tried to run away. But his hands and feet were tied down by thick ropes that strapped him to a cold stone slab. He tugged and pulled, but the ties wouldn't budge. Instead, his restraints just bit further into his wrists and ankles.

Panic laced its way through his body. There was no escape for him. Utterly helpless.

He noticed that his body was cloaked in a stark white toga. An absolute Greek Row cliche. Golden coins were strategically placed around his body. A dagger etched with Greek letters rested near his head.

A sudden blaze of light erupted in the center of the room. The crystal cup gleamed, resting on a pedestal. Next to it stood Alexandra—no, Alecto—and Meg.

They were both in their Fury forms. Faces twisted in pure malice. CiCi was on the other side, her expression serene and obedient, forming a triangle as she interpreted in ASL what Alecto was saying.

"Quiet down, everyone!" Alecto's voice was soft, but still managed to slice through the chanting, commanding immediate silence. She lifted the crystal cup like a piece of precious treasure, and together Meg and Alecto stalked toward Miles' sacrificial position. They moved in predatory unison. "The cup of Zeus," Alecto purred, "Shall hold the lifeforce of the sacrifice, displaying our undying promise of servitude."

Meg leaned over Miles' vulnerable form, her wings casting distorted shadows over him. He searched for a flicker of hope within her. Something that would tell him there was no way that she would go through with sacrificing him. But it was like the Meg he'd come to know wasn't in there anymore. Her eyes were completely devoid of the spark that Miles once found in them.

"You were just tricking me. Leading me on. Lying to me." The realization caused an ache to swell in Miles' chest. "You made me think I was crazy!" His voice cracked as the betrayal cut into him.

"Oh, Miles, haven't you ever played with your food before? It's really kind of the same thing." Meg's was disturbingly monotone. No emotion.

"That is *not* the same thing!" Miles spat at her, the words a mixture of fear and disgust.

"Look, I do like you. Really. I didn't lie to you about that. You're a fun guy." A crazed gleam surfaced in Meg's irises as she continued to speak. "But your purpose is so much bigger than simply being a frat boy. You are a *gift* to the gods!"

"I don't want to be a gift to the gods!" Miles shouted into the void of the chamber. "I want to go home!" Tears pricked at the corners of his eyes, but he would not let them fall. If this was going to be his ending, he wasn't going to give them the satisfaction of seeing him cry, but that didn't mean he wouldn't resort to begging. "*Please,*" he pleaded with Meg, trying to appeal to any sort of sympathy she may still have reserved for him. Desperation exuded from the sweat on his skin.

But his pleas fell on deaf ears as Meg ignored him and turned to her sister.

Alecto held up the goblet. "To the mighty gods of Olympus," her voice was thick with fanatical devotion,

"May their reign be eternal and their favor shine upon us!"

Meg grabbed the dagger and held it to Miles' throat, ready to slice him open from ear to ear.

Miles squeezed his eyes shut, not wanting to see his impending death.

"NO!" A voice shouted from across the room.

Miles snapped his eyes open to see Derek, his face determined, throw his cloak off and jump into action, lunging over to Typhon as fast as he could and stealing his sword out from under him. The room erupted into pure chaos as the shadowed figures surrounding the room began to take their hoods off as well. Familiar faces stuck out to Miles—girls from Omega Beta Mu and boys from Alpha Xi Pi. They all looked confused and scared, clearly realizing that this was not how the plan was supposed to go.

Meg and Alecto screeched as Derek charged at them with the stolen sword. They floated up toward the ceiling, watching in anger as Derek chopped through the ropes at Miles' hands and feet.

Freed from the slab, Miles stumbled, his muscles aching. Derek urgently helped Miles get his balance, and the two hobbled for the exit. But Typhon was already headed for them.

Derek grabbed Miles' arm. "Get out of here, dude!"

Before Miles could offer him any sort of thanks, Derek had already turned to face Typhon, who was now bearing down on them with a menacing snarl. To Miles' surprise, Derek stood his ground, his grip white knuckled around the hilt of the sword. "Go! Get out of here!" Derek shouted, leading Typhon away from the exit.

Miles tripped over his feet as he went to move. The drugs were still making him feel woozy. A strong arm slipped through his, helping him gain his footing. Miles was greeted by Phinn.

"Let's go!" Phinn spurred him on, and they raced as fast as they could out of the cavernous room.

The Furies' screams echoed behind them, but Phinn turned and slammed the door in their faces before they could get out of the room. He braced himself against the door, holding it shut, his muscles rippling beneath his cloak. "Quick, find me something to hold this!"

Miles didn't hesitate, doing as Phinn ordered. His mind raced, trying to recall their surroundings. He stared at the dark gray door, riddled with cracks.

Recognition dawned on him when he saw the etched gold filigree symbols. They were downstairs, across the hall from the Omega Beta Mu history room.

Without a word, Miles darted into the room. His eyes scanned the cluttered space, and he found what he needed. Grabbing a chair from the history room, Miles ran back to Phinn, huffing and puffing along the way, and watched as Phinn jammed the chair beneath the door.

"That should buy us a little more time. Come on." Phinn took Miles by the arm and dragged him up the stairs. Miles was trying his best to keep up, but, already feeling fatigued and trying to run in a toga with no shoes, he was having a difficult time.

As the boys sprinted up the stairs, a scream of terror rang out from behind them. It was Derek. It had to be him.

Miles shivered while he ran, thinking about what horrible things they would be doing to Derek for ruining the ritual.

When they finally made it outside, Miles was able to get Phinn to slow down just a little. They stopped for a quick breath in front of the hydra fountain.

"Wait, wait," Miles gasped, bent over, trying to get air. "What was all that? You and Derek knew about the whole sacrificing me thing?" He was furious.

"You have every right to be mad, but let me explain," Phinn reasoned.

"Explain then," Miles demanded.

Phinn let out an exasperated sigh. "Alexandra orchestrated your name being in the cup. She made sure that all the guys wrote down your name on the slip of paper."

"But why me?" It just didn't make sense.

"When I asked her, all she said was that you were the promised one. That everything would be explained at the ceremony. We thought it was innocent. We had no idea what they really had planned. That you were gonna be a sacrifice. We just figured it was one of those hazing rituals that you hear about on TV."

The promised one? Promised by whom?

Water from the fountain sprayed at them as the automatic timer switched it on.

Phinn's flushed cheeks turned pale. "Then, seeing you tied down to the slab with the dagger at your throat ... The whole thing is so twisted! I'm so sorry—"

A roar shook the ground they stood on as a reptilian tail swirled around Phinn's waist and lifted him up. While focused on their conversation, the boys hadn't paid attention to the fountain behind them. What used to be a fountain, anyway. It had come to life. Now the hydra was in full motion, swinging Phinn's flailing figure all over the place.

"Run, Miles!" Phinn screamed, and Miles bolted, running like he'd never run before.

Chapter Sixteen

Pieces of gravel and sticks took chunks out of Miles' heels as he ran through the woods. He figured that it was the safest place for him to run to because Alecto wasn't able to make it through the canopy last night. This was the moment, while he sprinted, that he finally let the tears stream down his cheeks. In one night, his whole life, all of his dreams, his friends, his first real crush, smashed on the pavement before him. Completely ruined.

He was going to need a lot of therapy in order to ever fully recover from this.

In the distance, Miles saw the main road. On the other side of the road, there was a large sign for a diner.

The sign read "Midnight Morsels: Where we cook up whatever you could possibly wish." Miles really wished for a way to call home and was hopeful that they would have a phone he could use.

A bell jingled as Miles made his way inside. He was instantly taken back in time when he stepped over the threshold. The floor was covered in a plush, purple velvet carpet with walls painted in a shimmering gold and silver hue. The lighting gave a mystical ambiance that created an enticing atmosphere. The tables were iridescent, as though they were carved out of pearl.

A beautiful woman came bustling out from the kitchen. Her hair, placed in a high ponytail, shimmered beneath the lights as her skin almost sparkled. "Hi, sweetie. How can I help ya?" She seemed busy as she handed out plates of food and mugs with coffee to other customers.

"I'm just wondering if I could use your phone?" Miles asked.

The woman peered at him from head to toe, narrowing her eyes at his bare feet and dirt-stained toga. "Lemme guess, you're from the college down the road?"

Miles sheepishly nodded.

She rolled her eyes in annoyance. "There's a pay phone by the bathroom. No funny business, okay?"

"Um, pay phone? Would you happen to have a quarter?" Miles felt bad for asking, but he pulled at the skirt of his toga to emphasize the fact that he had no money hiding anywhere.

The woman groaned, but she pulled out a shiny silver quarter from her apron. "You get one phone call, got it?"

He nodded and gave the woman his thanks.

Placing the quarter in the slot, Miles made the most important phone call of his life, silently praying, not to any Greek gods, that one of his parents would answer.

The rusty Dodge Caravan rounded the corner of the diner's parking lot. His dad was at the wheel, while his frantic-looking mom sat in the passenger's seat. The headlights shone across Miles, and his mom jumped out of the van as his dad put it into park.

"Miles, what in the world is going on? You sounded scared on the phone." His mom ushered Miles into the backseat of the van.

"I'll tell you everything, but can we get out of here first? I don't want them finding me." Miles glanced at the skies out the window, trying to see if Alecto or Meg were hunting for him. There were no shadowy figures to be found, though. The skies were quiet.

"You don't want who finding you?" his dad asked as he pulled away from the parking space.

That was when Miles went into all the details. All the events leading up to the ceremony. He came clean about Scylla attacking him in the pool. Char scaring him in the limo. Alecto swooping down on him and his friends at the basketball court. That they thought he was some "promised one."

When he was finished spilling his guts, his parents exchanged wary glances.

"And don't try to tell me that I'm crazy. All of this stuff happened. I'm not losing it. It's not just my imagination." Miles was talking at a fast pace, and then he slowed his speech to emphasize his next few words. "I will *not* be going back to Greek Row."

And then the Dodge Caravan made a turn, rounding the cul-de-sac to Greek Row.

Chapter Seventeen

"What are you doing?!" Miles demanded. "Did you not hear anything I told you? We need to get out of here before they come to sacrifice me!" Miles slapped at his dad's arm, trying to urge him to put the van back in gear and get the heck out of there.

The hydra fountain was back to stone. No sign of Phinn anywhere. Miles hoped he was okay. Hoped he was still *alive*.

His mom turned in her seat. "Honey, shh, shh," she calmly soothed. "We have to talk."

This was no time for talking. This was time for fleeing. He didn't understand why his parents were acting like this.

"Miles, honey, relax."

He ignored his mom. How could he relax? They'd just brought him back to the place where he was almost *murdered*.

"Your father and I need to tell you the truth."

Oh great. More truth.

"See, all those times we told you about how your father and I met in college, we weren't exactly truthful about the full story," she began, her voice wavering slightly. "Your father was part of Alpha Xi Pi, and I was in Omega Beta Mu. We dated all through college, and then when senior year hit, your father was chosen as Row Bachelor."

The weight of her words crashed down on Miles like an enormous wave threatening to tug him under.

"But we were so in love. Already planning our future together. So, I made a deal with the Furies and the gods. If they released your father as Row Bachelor, I'd give them my firstborn. And here you are. The full circle of your father and I's affection for each other. The embodiment of our sacrificial love. The promised one."

Miles recoiled as if struck. He couldn't believe what he was hearing. They had promised him—their own son—as a sacrifice before he was ever even born. Had they ever even seen him as their child? Did they only have Jesse as a way to replace Miles after he was gone? The truth was painful. He'd only ever been a means to an end for them. This wasn't sacrificial love at all. This was utter betrayal.

A talon tapped on the window of the Caravan, jolting Miles out of his own thoughts. Meg was standing outside the door, an unnerving grin spread across her face. It sent a chill up Miles' spine.

Miles' dad stepped out of the car, and his mom followed him.

Meg slid Miles' creaky door open. Gripping Miles' upper arm with a clawed hand, she ripped him out of his seat with incredible strength.

Alecto stepped up to his mom. "Daphne, great to see you again. You've aged ... well."

"And you haven't aged a bit, Alecto." His mom bowed her head toward Alecto. Bitterness filled Miles' mouth at the gesture.

His dad pointed toward Miles. "As promised, our firstborn. You'll be sure to remind the gods that we've followed through. They will bless us, right?"

Alecto clucked her tongue. "The gods are already aware of who Miles is. They are pleased with your offering, and as such, you shall be blessed."

Without another word to Miles, not even any sort of loving gesture like a hug or kiss, no apology, his parents got back in their van and drove away. On their way home to their son. Their *only* son.

Miles watched the taillights, hoping for them to turn bright red, his parents realizing what they'd done and coming back for him, but the red bulbs just grew smaller and smaller until they faded away completely.

"They aren't coming back," Meg stated blatantly.

"I just don't understand ..." Miles didn't even try to fight the Furies as they hauled him back to Omega Beta Mu.

"I told you before, Miles," Alecto spoke up, "Greek stories always end in tragedy."

Chapter Eighteen

Miles felt so alone. His family, which never felt like much of a family, had turned him over to be god fodder. And his friends were nowhere in sight, possibly already dead.

As Miles dragged his feet back to the chamber, his body becoming weighted lead, he felt like maybe he was ready to become the sacrifice he was meant to be. After all, in some roundabout way, he had always wanted popularity. Status. And now he was the Promised One. That sounded like a pretty popular title to him.

Everyone in the chamber was back at their posts, hoods on and prepared once again for the ritual that had been disrupted. Near Miles' deathbed slab, Derek and Phinn were restrained by Typhon's fire-breathing snakes. A sense of relief at seeing those two still alive, for now, flooded Miles.

"Miles!" Derek shouted when he saw him enter the dingy space. A snake sent a blast of heat in Derek's direction for the outburst. Miles could see the hope draining from Derek and Phinn's faces. They had wanted Miles to escape. They put their lives on the line trying to help him. They were the only ones who tried to give Miles a fighting chance. And Miles would be forever grateful for that.

"It's okay, guys." He gave them a weak smile.

There was the glint of a tear in Phinn's eye. "Love you, bro."

And then Derek burst into a fit of waterworks, his whole body shaking. He was saying something, but Miles couldn't make out any of the phrases. It brought a smile to his lips. Typical Derek.

"Oh my gods, will you three stop with the dramatics?" Alecto commanded.

"Yeah. You're ruining the vibe," Meg chimed in.

"Let's begin again. You know, before we were *rudely* interrupted," Alecto addressed the room, and the chants started up once again. Alecto cleared her throat.

"The cup of Zeus shall hold the lifeforce of the sacrifice, displaying our undying promise of servitude."

"Miles," Derek blubbered out, "Remember, *you only live twice.*" He nodded toward the crystal goblet in Alecto's claws as she continued.

"To the mighty gods of Olympus. May their reign be eternal and their favor shine upon us!"

Meg leaned her head down next to Miles', holding the dagger just beneath his chin.

Miles felt the sharp edge of the blade press against him. He saw Alecto shift the crystal goblet to catch the blood that was about to flow from him.

But instead of fear, Miles felt anger surge through him. Vengeance.

Derek was right. This wasn't how his story was going to end. He was the Promised One, for goodness' sake. In his eyes, he was promised to end the Row Bachelor ritual once and for all. No longer would anyone else become a sacrifice for the gods. Tragedy did not have to be a part of his tale.

Miles only hoped what he was about to do would work.

Using his head, he bashed into Meg's, aiming right for her crooked nose. There was a *crack,* and blood gushed from her nostrils. She screamed, dropping the dagger to grab her now busted face. With his cat-like reflexes, Miles swiped for the dagger before it could clatter to the ground. He flipped it, jumping up from his slab, and stabbed it right into Alecto's chest. The blade made a squelching sound as it entered her flesh. In pain and distracted, her taloned grip on the cup loosened, giving Miles the perfect opportunity to rip it from her grasp.

With the crystal cup in his hand, Miles scrambled to the other side of the room, placing his back against the wall and his sights on everyone around him.

Alecto and Meg composed themselves and sent fiery gazes toward Miles.

"Miles, give me the cup," Alecto demanded. In a furious state, she reached up and wrenched the dagger from her chest, tossing it to the ground. Blood seeped from the wound.

"No," Miles said.

Meg flipped her head in Typhon's direction.

Miles watched in horror as Typhon's snakes from hell wrapped around the throats of Phinn and Derek.

"You give us the cup or we kill your friends," Meg warned.

"Don't ... listen ... to ... her," Phinn croaked.

Meg sneered in their direction, and two more snakes coiled around their mouths, effectively keeping them shut.

Alecto threw out her hand. "I know you don't want their deaths on your hands. Give me the cup."

Miles shook his head no. They clearly wanted the cup, which made Miles realize that he was the one who had the control in the palm of his hand. And he wasn't about to give that control over to them. This was *his* epic Greek tale. His Odyssey.

"Hey, girls. Don't you know that all Greek stories end in tragedy?" And in one heroic gesture, Miles took the cup and slammed it to the ground, smashing the crystal into pieces.

"No!" Alecto and Meg screamed in horror. A rush of cold air and a blast of blinding light burst throughout the chamber. Miles watched as the light shifted into bolts, striking at Alecto, Meg, and Typhon, their very bones lighting up, zapping them to dust. It was like something straight out of an *Indiana Jones* movie.

Derek and Phinn fell to the ground. The rest of the onlookers ran from the chamber in terror.

Miles raced to his friends. "You guys alright?"

Both boys rubbed at their throats, and then Phinn spoke up. "Yeah, I'm good."

"Alright?! Alright?! Dude, that was freaking awesome!" Derek fist pumped the air. "You were like 'woah' then they were like 'woah' and then you delivered that sweet line and then KAPOW! Ashes."

Miles couldn't help but let out a laugh. "I think we need to get you some food. You sound deranged."

"You're probably right. But none of that food they got upstairs."

Phinn led the way to the exit. "Absolutely not. Maybe we could hit up a McDonald's. I could really go for a McHotDog."

Derek nodded vigorously. "Heck yeah!

While the boys made their way up the stairs, Miles' mind wandered. He thought about how Greek mythology was always labelled as fiction his whole life, only to have clawed its way into his reality. A shiver snaked its way down his spine as he wondered what other ancient nightmares and hungry legends were lurking just beyond the veil of their world, waiting in the dark for their turn to emerge from the shadows.

Bonus Chapter

Sing-song voices echoed loudly across the bus in a haunting, nursery-rhyme chorus as the wheels bounced beneath Phinn, throwing him forward. He bashed his face on the back of the seat in front of him.

"Beneath the boughs where evil plays,
Lurks a creature born of sin and fae.
Its borrowed face, so soft and sweet,
Hides hollow eyes of dark deceit.
Beware the Auf, pale and sly
A fake smile with teeth as sharp as knives.
It seeks a heart, warm and near,
To trade its place when night is here ..."

The song went on and on forever, laughter joining in every once in a while, practically making Phinn's eardrums bleed.

After the fiasco on Greek Row with his friends Miles and Derek, the three boys applied for as many jobs as they could. No longer being offered the benefits of gods, they were on their own when it came to paying their way for education. Which was the reason why when this job, being camp counselors, fell into their laps at a going rate of a $3,000 stipend for each of them, they couldn't pass up the opportunity. But if this was what summer camp was going to be like, Phinn was going to ask the bus driver to turn around and take him home right now.

Phinn rubbed the bridge of his nose, sore from hitting the seat in front of him.

Miles nudged his arm. "You okay? You look like you're gonna be car sick."

"The correct term is 'bus sick,'" Derek chimed in from the seat across from them.

Phinn rolled his eyes. "When we signed up for this, I thought everyone would be a lot less … annoying." He craned his neck to look at all the benches, the kids proudly wearing their yellow "Camp Clover Lake" t-shirts that got mailed out a week prior. None of them looked out of place in their shirts. Except Phinn. His tanned skin and inky long hair made him feel like he stuck out. It brought him back to a time in middle school when kids who reminded him of the kids on this bus used to bully him. He couldn't believe that it still bothered him to this day. Especially when he was in charge of these kids. It's not like they'd be picking on him. He wasn't in middle school anymore.

The open window next to Derek blew his orange hair in every direction. "They aren't annoying. They're kids. You just aren't used to all this yet. Don't worry. Once we get to the camp, you're gonna have the time of your life!" Derek popped some PopRocks into his mouth, cracking his jaw open just a smidge so that he could hear the candy crackle.

Phinn was glad someone was confident about them having a good time.

He turned around. Looking over the back of his seat, he saw that there wasn't a single child not joining in on the song. "What exactly *is* an auf?" Phinn asked Miles, knowing that ever since Greek Row, Miles had been going down the rabbit hole of all sorts of myths and legends. He was surprised that Miles was even able to get in that much research while living on Derek's couch in his basement. As far as Phinn knew, Miles still hadn't let his parents know that he was even still alive. That their sacrificial offering didn't stick. He wondered how long it would be before they noticed something was wrong. How long it would take for them to realize they weren't in the gods' favor.

Miles' eyes lit up at Phinn's question, like he'd been waiting for him to ask it this whole entire ride. "An auf is—" but before he could finish, Miles let out a blood-curdling scream ...

To be continued in

Coming 2027

Acknowledgments

As a late arrival to the 90s (1996, baby!), I owe my sister endless thanks for giving me a proper 90s childhood. From filling our Lite-Brite with the brightest colors, to making sure our Betty Spaghettys were best friends, and solving mysteries alongside Mary-Kate and Ashley, she's given me memories I'll always treasure. I don't know where I'd be without her, and I'm grateful every day for her support and advice throughout my life.

Thank you to Mad Axe Media for reading my pitch and seeing something in it. I'll forever be grateful for this opportunity.

And finally, to my readers—and to anyone who has ever carried the weight of something they didn't choose—thank you for being here. Life is sometimes a bit of a Greek tragedy. But there is hope in knowing the past does not have to define the future. Rewrite your story, and don't be afraid to create a little chaos tearing down the ancient monsters along the way.

About the author

AudraKate Gonzalez, the evil mastermind-er, author-writes YA Horror for kids/young adults who love horror and are looking for something to keep them up at night. She lives in Ohio with her handsome husband and her adorable furry bad boys, Zero and Scrappy Doo. When AudraKate isn't writing, you can find her reading, watching scary movies or sleeping. You can follow AudraKate on Instagram and TikTok @lets.get.lit.erature

Don't miss these titles from

Avalable now!

Paperback ISBN:
979-8-990685-82-6

Paperback ISBN:
978-1-966497-00-4

Paperback ISBN:
978-1-966497-02-8

Paperback ISBN:
978-1966497-04-2

Paperback ISBN:
978-1-966497-14-1

And coming soon...

Paperback ISBN:
978-1-966497-27-1
October 13th, 2026

www.ingramcontent.com/pod-product-compliance
Lightning Source LLC
LaVergne TN
LVHW040059080526
838202LV00045B/3709